THE EXQUISITE CORPSE

A NOVEL BY

Alfred Chester

AFTERWORD BY

Diana Athill

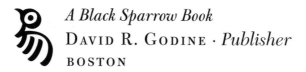

A Black Sparrow Book

DAVID R. GODINE · *Publisher*

BOSTON

This is
A Black Sparrow Book
published in 2003 by
David R. Godine, Publisher
Post Office Box 450
Jaffrey, New Hampshire 03452
www.blacksparrowbooks.com

First published in 1967 by Simon & Schuster, New York

The afterword has been adapted by Diana Athill
from her book *Stet: A Memoir*, and is published here
by kind permission of Grove/Atlantic, Inc.

The Black Sparrow Books pressmark is by Julian Waters
www.waterslettering.com

LIBRARY OF CONGRESS
CATALOGING-IN-PUBLICATION DATA
Chester, Alfred 1928–1971
The exquisite corpse : a novel / by Alfred Chester ;
afterword by Diana Athill.
p. : cm.
ISBN 1-57423-197-9 (pbk. : alk. paper)
1. Gay men — Fiction. 2. Body, Human — Fiction. I. Title
PS3505.H679 E97 2003
813'.54 22   2003061123

Printed in the United States of America

For Dris Ben Hussein El Kasri
For Dris Kasri
For Dris
For You—whatever your name is and whoever you are
—with love and admiration

THE EXQUISITE CORPSE

1

On his way across the attic, John Anthony passed the bassinet and in a bit of looking glass that showed among the rags he saw the stranger's face. It was so unexpected that the hair on his head stood up and the breath went out of him. He threw a hopeless look over his shoulder, but of course no one was there. His eyes felt bruised.

Gathering his courage, John Anthony bent over the bassinet and cleared away the pretty rags until the whole of the hand-mirror with its heavy gilt frame lay exposed. He stared into the brown eyes, studied the unhappy face, and began whimpering.

"You will make me crazy," he said, putting his fists to his temples.

Then, as the tears streamed down his cheeks, he

hugged himself and moaned, "Poor baby, poor. Poor poor baby. Baby poor poor."

And then, with a burst of ferocious anger, he grabbed the mirror out of the bassinet and flung his fierce chin against it. He bellowed through the empty house: "Why? Why must I suffer your destiny?"

2

Noon in the garment district, the sunny streets swarming with hungry people. Joy swam in the air, as did lint, clots of fur and multicolored fuzz. Even Baby Poorpoor, lost for a moment in the appetite and freedom of the mob, was happy. He mingled, smiling, and fell in love with everyone he saw—the slender secretaries, the strong boys pushing racks of summer dresses, the manufacturers with tiny puffs of hair sticking out of their ears and nostrils.

No one looked at him or loved him back, but he didn't mind until a cloud passed across the sun, turning everything gray. Then his rapture darkened. He grew sad, though not bitter, and very tired suddenly. It was exhausting not to be loved back. Maybe if he gave his hair a blond rinse? Or lost some weight, say fifty pounds? Maybe if he stole or begged enough money to buy a pair of haunting-blue contact lenses and threw away these flaring pockmarked (from where the rhinestones had fallen out) tortoise shells that used to belong to his mother? Baby heaved a long painful sigh, frightening himself because the sound came from such depths.

Through the crowds, he saw on the opposite side of the street a man he thought might be his younger brother. Baby ducked through a doorway and, pressing himself against the stamped tin wall, watched the man move off toward Seventh Avenue. Had he been seen? He imagined his brother sitting down to supper that night, spreading a napkin across his lap and telling his wife and children, "I saw him. Not far from Seventh Avenue. He ran into a hallway and hid there."

Around their beautiful table sagging with food, the family received the news, each in his own way. One of them tittered. One roared with laughter. One blushed. One sneered. And then they all began talking about him so loud and so long and so cruelly that he didn't at first realize there was someone standing next to him in the hallway.

"Julie . . ." she whispered.

He jumped in surprise, then turned his head cautiously to the left. A woman with red hair as coarse as wool had her bloodshot eyes close to him.

"You better come back to me now, Julie."

She was definitely crazy and perhaps even dangerous. You never could tell in New York which maniac was or wasn't homicidal. Too scared to look down at her hands and see if she held a pistol or a knife, Baby spoke to her eyes.

"No, no," he said. "I'm not Julie."

"Come on, darling," she urged, pinching his arm. She wore torn white gloves but evidently had no weapons. "Let's go now."

"No." He pulled his arm away.

The woman's painted eyebrows snapped up almost to her hairline. "All right then. Don't say I didn't warn you."

She stormed past him and crossed the street, ignoring the crowds, the dress racks, the traffic. She was wearing a white picture hat and an orange dress.

Half a block away, on the other side of the street, a cop appeared from around the corner. He and the woman were heading toward each other.

Baby came to his senses, bolted from the building and ran the other way.

3

The window shades were down and everything was red, since only the little maple lamp was on, the little lamp with the torn red paper shade. The room was hot and flushed and feverish. It smelled of iodine and Lysol, and also of loose metallic shit. Only the old man's hands and head were outside the sheet when Xavier sat down at the edge of the bed. He had been in a coma for the past week and his face looked mummified. His gnarled hands lay palms up next to his ears which had come to seem very big. The hands simply lay there, palms up, scaly and twisted.

The sheet was almost flat against the bed except for the feet and the lump of squirming rubber bag. Having sewn up Papa's anus, the doctors had cut a slit in his belly and hauled out a length of intestine to detour the excrement. Xavier carefully folded back the sheet until the body lay exposed as far as the gray pubic hair. He shuddered. A lot of intestine was visible. It was a raw red thing, thrilling red, as red as sores. Studying it, Xavier believed that few civilized men could actually contain, could be capable of, so raw red an interior. But Papa had been born a peasant on the shores of the Black Sea. Worst of all about the intestine was, it seemed somehow alive. Terribly, spontaneously alive, and with an exotic domineering will all its own. It looked dangerous, invincible.

Xavier put a finger to Papa's belly but pulled it back at once because the squirming increased, becoming violent. The intestine shot suddenly out of the rubber bag. It spun like the nozzle of a garden hose, flailing and lashing, spraying watery turds every which way around the room. Before Xavier had the presence of mind to jump up, the pale blue wallpaper, the ceiling, the bedclothes, the air, Papa and he himself were drenched with shit.

"Mama, Mama, come quickly!" he cried.

Calmly pulling on her rubber gloves, Mama entered, undismayed by the shower. She talked gently to the intestine, wooed it. Her white hair turning brown, she tried to reason with it, humor it, joke with it, perhaps love it a little as she had never loved Papa. And so, before long, it was flopping around tamely, and Mama shoved it back into the rubber bag.

Then she scrubbed up and disinfected the room. She

washed Papa and changed the sheets. Xavier didn't help
her; he stood in the doorway feeling dirty and nauseous.
When Mama was done, she took her rags, mop and
bucket, and soon Xavier heard her in the living room
moving the squeaky chair to the old kidney-shaped
desk. One by one she would now phone all her children
at their various homes and offices to tell them of her
sorrow.

Xavier sat down again, and again he lowered the
sheet. Below the emaciated ribcage with its skin like
hairy parchment. Below the throbbing red bag. Should
he lower it further? He had never seen his father's genitalia and imagined them as rich and fruity. Could he
lower it? No, he didn't dare.

Warily, he put his hand out, but the intestine didn't
object to his finger now. Xavier doodled thoughtfully,
then wrote: WARM EVENING SPRING.

4

The elevated line was the most ancient structure in the neighborhood, except for the trees. It dated from Medieval Times or even earlier, was dark and grimy, clotted with eternity and grease, austere. Yet it could also be voluptuous as when the fast new trains flashed their brief blue lightning across the tracks. Then the El shook and shimmied hotly, and melting grease clots ran down the girders to the street.

It spanned a wide bleak avenue and threw a cast of perpetual night. Everything in its shadow—the tenements, the antique beauty parlor, the cemetery, the gasoline station left from another age, the squat ruined factories—was shut either forever or until morning, which would never come. What thrived was wild empty space, unused space that no one wanted or had ever wanted except cats and rusting cans and tall weeds and lust and scum bags and lunatics and ghosts and tremendous niggers with their flies open and knives or nightmare cocks sticking out. As Xavier walked along that dark street, his knees rattled and his asshole twitched. And overhead a train came through, roaring with sex. Xavier looked up at the pale passing faces framed in the lighted windows. They too were roaring with sex.

On one corner of the avenue was a candy store. He went into it now and sat down in one of the two booths. It was an old-fashioned candy store and the booths were made of heavy polished wood and worn stuffed leather, its soda fountain covered with marble, its light spreading from two glass balls suspended by brass stems from the ceiling. The store stayed open all night, throughout the perpetual night.

The owner had a large fat wife whose pretty little face was buried in flesh. She wore round steel-rimmed glasses that doubled the size of her eyes. She had a massive ramplike bosom. She tended the store all day and he all night. He was handsome in a wounded, beaten, frightened way. He looked as if thick drops of maraschino-flavored blood trailed behind him wherever he went. He wasn't short but he gave that impression, perhaps because his wife's huge phantom was always overpoweringly present.

Xavier couldn't remember a time when the little man and the big woman hadn't been there, more or less the same. The owner was sitting now on one of the stools at the fountain reading the book section of the Sunday *Times*. It was a Saturday night, or rather Sunday morning. They had never spoken to each other except as customer and shopkeeper, but a switchboard of invisible feelings kept their eyes from ever connecting. How nice it would be, Xavier told himself, if tonight, just for once, in a brotherly way their eyes met and the man put aside the newspaper, lifted his apron, dropped his pants and let Xavier rest his cheek in the warm wounded crotch.

He lowered the newspaper and asked Xavier what he wanted. Xavier wanted a banana split but out of embarrassment ordered a butterscotch sundae instead. The man made it badly. The woman made everything better, more generously. Her flesh shook and opened as she scooped up and flung down the balls of ice cream, the chopped walnuts, the syrups and sauces. The man turned pink as he began mildly tossing the whipped-cream bomb. He tossed without much energy, while his wife gave wild heaves and ho's, lavishly, with all her quivering body. When the cream came shooting out, he turned bright red and there were tears in his bashfully lowered eyes, so darkly lashed.

5

Papa's voice flew disembodied through the rosy air, filling up the room. It came out of practically nowhere, virtually nothing, but it was complete, manly, full.

"I asked Mama to send you in because I have something to say to you."

Xavier tried to control his trembling. Why should this mummy want to speak to him? What right did it have to crumble out of its silence and ask him in for an oracular chat? Too horrible! Never in all those years before the coma had Papa ever held a conversation with him. And now when death should already have consumed him, he woke, or his voice woke, dripping with the weeds of antiquity.

"Maybe I didn't seem to be a loving father, but I always loved you very much, very very much, very deeply. Do you believe me?"

Xavier stopped trembling. "No," he said, not only because he didn't, but because he was suspicious of the coma and even of the cancer, and wasn't sure that Papa would ever die—in which case a romantic reconciliation was not something Xavier wanted to carry into the cold indifferent future.

Papa sighed and his bones clattered. The intestine farted frequently, a splurting and muted but angry noise. Xavier closed his attention on the lump in the sheet so as not to have to be the next one to speak.

However, the silence between them persisted for so long that Xavier finally glanced up at his father's eyes. They were shut. He couldn't remember whether they had been open before, but assumed they must have been, and so decided that Papa had slid back into his coma as casually as he had slid out of it. He wasn't dead. At least, the intestine wasn't dead.

Xavier, who had been sitting on a chair beside the bed, stood up.

"Where are you going?"

"Nowhere. My underwear got caught in my ass."

He sat down. Papa's eyes were still closed, or perhaps they were very slightly, imperceptibly open, a crack through which the eons peered. In any case, Xavier now knew he could be seen.

"Not everyone is lucky enough to be able to say openly how they feel in their hearts. Some people have to keep their hearts hidden."

So this is what Papa was like after all? Chilly, unfriendly Papa? Of course Xavier had often seen him crying when they all sat together at the movies; but heartless people always cried at the movies.

"Maybe you're too young to understand that."

"To understand what?"

"That some people have to hide their feelings."

Xavier said, "Maybe I'm one of them."

Did Papa know that until an hour ago he had been in a coma? Xavier wanted to ask because there was another pause in the conversation, but he changed his mind. The question seemed too personal.

"And now it's too late," Papa said.

"What is?"

"Everything. Maybe I'll be dead tomorrow."

Xavier glanced at his own little alarm clock on his own little night table under his own little maple lamp alongside his own little bed. Papa was dying in Xavier's room because it was quieter there. The master bedroom faced on the street and collected the noises of people and traffic. Xavier slept with Mama. (Many years later, when Xavier was a middle-aged man, he went mad in a tropical country, and his lunacy centered around the belief that Papa had died for him, instead of him, literally in his place.)

"It's a quarter after seven," Xavier said.

A long time passed before Papa spoke. "In the morning?"

"Now? No, it's evening."

"Try to remember me with love."

"Yes, Papa."

"There are some other things I must say to you." Pause. "If you have the time, Dickie."

"Xavier!" Xavier cried.

"Let me call you Dickie."

"If you do, I'll leave this room. *My* room."

Papa sighed again. It sounded like wind hooting through catacombs, and Xavier, once more in the presence of the ancients, held himself rigid so as not to start trembling.

"Xavier . . ."

"What?"

"I have tried to raise you to be a good man. I wanted life to be easier for you than it's been for me. Maybe I should have shown you my feelings more, but nobody is perfect. In my time people didn't wear their hearts on their sleeves. I hope you'll always be a good boy and remember your Papa. God will bless you for it as he blessed me for remembering Grandpa. Do you remember Grandpa, my little son?"

"I remember his teeth in a glass of water that had a cut rose in it. I also remember that he died in his sleep in a room on the Lower East Side and that no one found him for days."

"Nothing else?"

"No, well—he was very hairy and he wore black clothes all the time."

"At home, in the old country, he was a rabbi."

"Ah, yes. I think I'd heard that."

"I hope you'll say Kaddish for me. Do you know what that is, Dickele?"

"Xavier! Xavier!"

The intestine screamed with hysterical abandon like a woman in the night. Papa's eyes blew wide open: they were deep blue, almost purple, perhaps because of the redness in the room. Xavier had never looked into his father's eyes before, and so had never noticed the color.

"What was that scream?" Papa asked.

"I suppose it was Mrs. Ferguson next door. Her husband must be beating her up again. He's out of jail."

They listened, but only muted fartings reached their ears.

"It used to be a good neighborhood," Papa said. "Things like that didn't happen." His eyes closed. "I'm tired. Ask Mama to come in."

Xavier stood up gratefully.

"Goodbye . . . Xavier. Try to remember me with love."

6

T. S. Ferguson traveled the subway during rush hour so that as many people as possible would fall in love with him at once. In the creepy blue light of the mobbed and clattering trains, he ran from carriage to carriage, rolling his eyes and wrinkling his nose and tossing his thrilling black hair. He spread through the tunnels like perfume or like a rumor of catastrophe on earth. People tracks away grew uneasy, confused. Whole stations quivered.

Half of a dead cigar between his teeth, Ferguson entered, drove his way into, a train as one from another world, promising the crowd more than his handsome face and powerful body. He sparked off an explosion through the grim dirty air. He promised the end of daily life, interminable ecstasy, something new at last. The passengers could barely catch their breath, keep their hands to themselves, contain their swollen tongues, resist the lurch and pounding of their blood. Newspapers and magazines slipped out of helpless fingers asking only to be no longer homeward bound. Whatever joy or suffering a moment ago awaited the passengers at the end of their journey now lay in a crumpled dirty heap along with chewing gum and newspapers on the carriage floor.

Ferguson's dark lashes rose and fell, making secret assignations with everyone.

"Fuck me, fuck me," the whispered incantation followed him through the train. And he smiled back his wordless rendezvous. Ten o'clock in the lot behind the supermarket. Or under the bridge.

He slew without mercy as he passed, yet all gave him thanks.

Ferguson stood alone in the wind and the sunset on an elevated platform, the red twilight crashing around him.

The trains were less crowded now. His shoes felt heavy on his feet. He climbed up out of the subway and walked the sad windy streets to the parking lot. With a slump, he got into his car. Wearily, he drove the broad boring highway home.

Ferguson lived in autumn. There was a smell of

smoke in the air. The big harmless trees had yellow leaves and the neat lawns were rusty. There was a tartness in the breeze as if God had dropped a twist of lemon peel into it. Ferguson had a pretty white house with two pillars on the porch, a large garden, three children and a wife.

"Tom! You look so tired, honey. Was it a terribly hard day? You stayed awfully late."

As usual, he was shot through the heart when he crossed the threshold and, clutching his torn chest, he fell to the floor, staggering a little so that he landed on the rug. The children crawled all over him, screaming with laughter. Andy sat down on his crotch and Ferguson started getting a hard on which Mrs. Ferguson noticed. The game ended.

She put the kids to bed while Ferguson dragged himself to his easy chair, turned on the television and poured a milk and whiskey from the decanter on the side-table. Presently supper was served with wine and candlelight and a log on the fire. The Fergusons chatted to each other affectionately about their day. After the cheese and fruit there was the last act of *Don Giovanni* on the phonograph, a little more television, then a book, and bed.

Ferguson switched off the light and turned away from his wife. He loved her, but after a long day at the office and on the overcrowded subway system, he was tired. The linen sheets grew hot and soggy with her waiting. Steamy. He imagined the enormous paramecium breaking loose from between her legs, floating free, stalking the dark room wretchedly as it wrung its ciliae and pleaded.

Sleepily, Ferguson stroked himself, giving off a noise of pleasure. All over the world people were in love with him, their heads filled with his frenzy. Everywhere people waited in the ten o'clock shadows for him to appear. He touched his thighs for them and his tough hairy belly. He opened his mouth and a thousand tongues entered. At last, seizing with both hands the whole of its massive splendor, he squeezed his cock and heard a universal panting. To fulfill mankind, and because he loved her, he rolled himself over twice and without even aiming came to a stop inside Mrs. Ferguson.

7

On a sunny afternoon, snug in a blue-and-gold wind-breaker that had JAMES MADISON H. S. in felt letters on the back—like all his clothes the jacket was a present from John Anthony—Baby Poorpoor went to Coney Island. Since there were cops around, he crossed Surf Avenue in a hurry, trying to be inconspicuous. Cops always questioned him, though he never did anything wrong. They would come up to him for no reason at all and ask where he was going or what he was intending to do. He never had a ready answer, and so appeared suspicious even to himself. Why did the police question him? Baby didn't know, but he had finally come to believe it was against the law to be, to look like Baby Poorpoor.

He sneaked down behind Nathan's, in among the shady alleys and the boarded-up shacks. There his pace slowed. He liked it here. He even liked the solitude. Old merry-go-round music left from old summers haunted the lanes, was louder at corners where it rose on the wind. Catching a phrase here and there, Baby hummed as he walked.

He reached the boardwalk and, like the perverts, maniacs and murderers he had heard about in his childhood, he went underneath it rather than on top. The smell was marvelous: a mixture of sweetly rotting planks, cold dark sand, torn sneakers, rotting jockstraps and shade which never vanished except for a few minutes before sunset. People strolled overhead, their heels squeaking, clumping and clattering, but Baby wasn't afraid—or only very little. He wandered around under the boardwalk, kicking the sand, hoping to find something. Anything. A skull, a diamond, a lover, a condom, a letter, a murdered man. A thread he could follow into a new life.

But he found nothing and soon the mysterious hope left him. He went down the bright beach to the water's edge and seated himself just beyond the reach of the waves. The cold sand chilled his ass. The world was blue and gold but no words were written on the back of it. Nothing that met Baby's gaze had been made by man, and he was enchanted by the strangeness of this thought. He sat, watching the waves draw closer.

A cloud passed over the sun and everything sagged. Water, sand and sky collapsed like paper bags. Baby remembered with a pang and a chill that the hour would roll into night. Closing his eyes, he waited for the sun to inflate him again.

At the railing on the boardwalk, T. S. Ferguson stood with his hand shielding his eyes and a loud knocking in his head. It wasn't so much the bloated solitary figure on the beach that excited him as the writing on the windbreaker. Moments of glory, though they were common to him, made Ferguson feel faint. In fact, he was so giddy now that he had to put both hands on the railing, for all the corners of his life seemed to lift flaming and to curl inward in a single miraculous fire.

When he recovered his strength, he raced down the boardwalk stairs.

At first he merely circled around Baby Poorpoor. Then, growing bolder, he muttered and stared. Then he bared his teeth and began hissing. He hissed and snarled, walking in a circle while the sun went red for setting.

Baby broke into a cold sweat and his eyeglasses misted over, which was just as well, for if this madman was going to kill him, he didn't want to watch it happening.

Ferguson spoke through the fog: "I condemn you to be James Madison."

To be anything other than Baby was such a relief that Baby smiled and relaxed. He took his glasses off and squinted at the blurred man in the business suit who he knew could mean him nothing but harm.

8

John Doe arrived at the apartment at twilight, just as everything turned blue, a big brown paper bag in his arms. He kicked the door shut behind him, then stood in the middle of the room, his face screwed up with rage.

"You shouldn't really make those faces, Johnnie," James Madison scolded in order to hide his pleasure. He lay on a cot next to the open window, and he was naked except for a pink brassiere and a pair of yellow panties. "I once heard about a man whose face got stuck that way and he became terrible to look at."

"All right, Cleopatra. No one asked you. And don't call me Johnnie."

"Why not? What should I call you then?"

"You don't have to call me anything. There are only two of us here."

He set the paper bag down on the bridge table and tore it open rather ferociously. He took out a candle which he lit at once and stuck into some old wax on a corner of the bridge table.

"That makes the room look very pretty," James Madison said. "We could use some more furniture though. Does that icebox in the kitchen work? I mean, the refrigerator. I tried getting it on today but nothing happened."

"What do you need it for?"

"I guess I don't *really* need it, but—"

"I never had the gas or electricity turned on, and I don't intend to now. And no one ever complained before."

"Oh."

John Doe lit a cigar from the candle flame, then took a container of milk from the bag. There were already a couple of whiskey bottles on the bridge table, also three glasses.

"I washed the glasses today," James Madison said, and then, while John Doe mixed himself a drink, he asked, "Do you have an ulcer?"

"None of your business." He seemed very nervous. "Why, is my shit black again?"

The question caught James Madison by surprise, embarrassed him slightly. How should he know the color of John Doe's shit? They'd only met the day before. He hadn't even seen him naked; he hadn't even seen his cock. They hadn't even kissed. So he said, "Do people with ulcers have black shit?"

"It depends. Sometimes. If the ulcer—" He became suddenly angry. "Now, will you stop that, damn it! I don't want any personal questions, you hear? There's nothing personal going on here and you better get that into your head right off."

"I'm sorry," James Madison said, blushing all over his body.

"There are some cans of food in the bag and some pills. If you get bored, take a few pills. They won't hurt you. Did you try those red ones I gave you last night?"

"I haven't been bored a bit. I cleaned the place up, maybe you noticed."

"Well, if you get bored, take a few. You can take them one on top of the other if you like, like a pousse-café. And don't go running in and out of the apartment. Stay put. You hear?"

"Where would I go?"

"Don't go anywhere. I wouldn't like the neighbors wondering what kind of freaks live here. I've also brought some toilet paper to wipe shit and blood and come with. Oh, and a few Tampax." He slid the box out of his pocket and tossed it on the cot.

Although James Madison felt wounded that he had been referred to as a freak by the man who was presumably his lover, he feigned a giggle while he opened the half-empty box. "What are these for?"

"Your period."

"My *what?*"

"Are you deaf on top of everything else?"

James Madison said, "When does my period happen?"

"Right now. Start shoving."

"Dry?" he asked, rolling down his panties. "I hope I don't have to put them in dry. Do I?"

"You do."

There were two wooden chairs in the room, and John Doe sat down on one of them. He crossed his legs, sipped his drink, puffed his cigar, and grew excited watching James Madison struggle with the Tampax. He fondled himself from crotch to knee.

"One night," he said, "I'm going to—what are you stopping for?"

"It hurts."

"You idiot! Didn't you take the wrapper off?"

"Of course I did. It hurts anyway." He added slyly, "It might not hurt as much if you helped me."

"That's what you think. Get going!"

James Madison flung his legs up in the air again. "Am I supposed to insert them one after the other or one alongside the other?"

"I—hmmm . . ." John Doe was unsure. "One next to the other I think would be more picturesque."

After much huffing and puffing, and a few bravely muffled cries, James Madison groaned. "Dear God in heaven! There, that's the second one in. I wonder what I look like."

"You look good. You look good enough to eat. Does it hurt?"

James Madison was so flattered he couldn't speak. He shook his head.

"It'll hurt when you've got all four in. Space, I need space, and a lot of it, because I . . . am . . . really . . . BUILT . . . BIG."

"Come on, let's see it," James Madison said, surprising himself with his boldness.

"You'll see it when I'm good and ready." He looked at his watch and stood up. "When I come back here tomorrow or the day after, I want to see all four of those Tampax in place. Is that clear?"

"You're not going already, are you?"

John Doe straightened his tie in silence, smoothed his hair back and left the apartment, locking the door behind him.

James Madison listened to the heavy footsteps fading down the stairs. He wanted to get up and eat something, or at least go to the toilet. But, full of John Doe, he lowered his legs, turned carefully onto his left side, and looked dreamily out the window. An incinerator in one of the projects down the street erupted and a host of orange sparks shot into the sky. The sparks rose, then softly fell; a million cascading stars; and his contented heart thanking each and every one of them, James Madison fell asleep.

9

While climbing the stairs, his rage turned suddenly to terror. He stopped walking and maneuvered the paper bag away from his chest so that it wouldn't crackle so much. What waited for him?

He listened, through the hallway and the house and out in the street, but he heard only his own harsh breathing which seemed to roar through his nose. He held his breath and went on climbing, almost on tiptoe. The upper stories had a touch of gold to them, for the late afternoon light fell through the open trap in the roof and transformed the sagging, broken stairs and the rusty iron banisters. There was something of a fairy tale about it, and it added to his apprehension. A dozen hammers knocked at his heart.

He stood listening outside the door. His balls were tight and there was a sore feeling in his duodenum. Slowly, he turned the knob. The door was locked.

I want to go home. Please God let me go home.

In reverie he saw Mrs. Ferguson and her three freckled cowboys standing on the porch. They were all laughing and shouting as Daddy came up the flagstone path. Daddy's plain innocent face was all smiles, though he was sweaty and tired from his long day at the office. He waved to his innocent family. If John Doe went through the door in front of him, would he ever be able to impersonate Ferguson again? Wouldn't the children know he was an impostor boiling with envy of their happy lives?

Shifting the bag, he took the key from his pocket and pushed it in the lock.

The room was golden, its stillness dreadful.

On the floor near the bed lay James Madison in his brassiere and panties. His head hung over a white enamel basin still filling with blood. His throat was cut open, and entwined among the fingers of his out-stretched hand was a switchblade knife. It looked as though he had been dead a long time, a very long time, perhaps always. This look of permanence soothed John Doe and freed him from his terror. The room, the whole tenement, the street, in fact the world had all been built with the naked suicide inside it. The bloody basin and the tumbled head had been scratched on fate's blue-print. What did it have to do with John Doe? What had he been so afraid of?

He shut the door quietly behind him, and gently, gently went across the room, setting the paper bag down on the table.

10

Mary Poorpoor was only a child herself when her son was conceived. She was unmarried and alone in the world. She was homeless, hungry and skinny. She had no idea who the father could be, but it came to pass that she hoped more and more it was the kindly fat social worker who befriended her a few months after she became pregnant. The social worker was named Emily, and she set Mary up in a sunny tenement flat that had its own toilet as well as a bathtub in the kitchen, heat and hot water. Emily was a stately-looking sober yet playful woman with large breasts under either or both of which she was given to hiding one-dollar bills.

"I've got a little something for you," she liked to say

upon entering their apartment in the evening. "But it's up to you to find it—or them. Yes, maybe even *them*."

Sometimes Mary rummaged around for hours in Emily's clothing and under the folds of flesh and among all the sticky hairs before she would finally, and with a cry of triumph to hide her disappointment, locate the money. One or two one-dollar bills. Never a cent more.

Each day, when the treasure hunt was over, Emily would toss her hair over her face, howl like a wolf, beat her chest like a gorilla and say, "Now, Little Red Riding Hood, I'm going to eat you up."

"No, no no," Little Red Riding Hood would cry in fright, but she was so tiny and the wolf so strong that there was really no alternative to surrender. Besides, if the truth were told, despite her pique over Emily's cheapness, Mary enjoyed being eaten. It made her feel electrocuted.

One hot spring morning, after Emily had gone to work, Baby was born. Mary awoke from a happy dream in which she had been relieving herself after months of constipation and lo! there was the child whimpering between her legs. As she didn't know how to disengage him from her body, the young mother lay waiting for the social worker to arrive.

Baby had a pretty face, but Mary was horrified to see that he was rather brown in skin color. How could she ever explain this to Emily? During the course of the day, however, Mary remembered the time that she and Emily had played with the frankfurters and thus was more convinced than ever that Emily was indeed Baby's father. This made her soul rejoice. Since Baby's skin looked dry and dirty, Mary sprinkled him now and again from the watering can on the window ledge beside her bed. There were many healthy and flourishing plants on the ledge and out on the fire escape as well, for Mary Poorpoor had a green thumb.

By the time Emily arrived the child was the size of a large watermelon, but brownish.

"Well, well, what have we here?" said the social worker.

"Your son," Mary whispered, blushing.

"Ours," Emily said.

They looked into each other's eyes for a long time. Then Emily cut the child away. She always carried a switchblade in her purse, for her work took her into dangerous neighborhoods. She knotted Baby's umbilical cord, snapped back his long foreskin, washed his mother's cunt out, changed the bedclothes, wrapped Baby in a blanket and put him to Mary's bosom.

"There's no mistaking that he's your son," Mary said, gazing down ecstatically at the eager little mouth.

"Nor yours either," said Emily.

Thereupon, the delighted parents embraced with such fervor that Baby, caught between them, screamed. They kissed, hugged each other, and sang love songs until late in the night. Surely, they were the happiest family on earth, so perhaps the gods were jealous, because tragedy flew in upon them just one week later.

There was another hot morning collapsing among the tenements and the thin pale trees, and Mary was bitterly cleaning her apartment. She had imagined that after Baby was born she would find something more than one-dollar bills under her husband's breasts. But it hadn't turned out that way, and Mary was beginning to feel nasty about it. She longed for pretty clothes and richer food, and she thought it would be wise to put something aside for the future.

While his mother pondered bitterly, Baby slept in a wicker basket that hung from the ceiling by ropes. Emily had devised this ingenious cradle to keep the rats and the roaches from attacking her son.

Suddenly Mary heard a whirring sound and she turned just in time to see two winged creatures come flying through the window and land on their toes in the middle of the room. Since she knew at once that they were fairies, she wasn't afraid but enchanted. They had lovely delicate white faces with sharp dimples and long blond hair. They were pretty enough to be movie stars. At first glance Mary thought they were naked, but she then realized they were wearing long transparent gowns that shimmered when they moved. Under their gowns they had little breasts, much like her own, beneath which, Mary sadly reflected, money could not have been hidden. Their wings were of bubbly frosted glass like toilet windows. One of the fairies carried a squirming something wrapped in an old army blanket.

"Do not be afraid of me, Mary Poorpoor," the fairies sang in one single crystal voice as their toes touched the floor. "I have come with a blessing for you."

"You have?" exclaimed Mary happily. "What is it?"

"I am going to give you my child in exchange for yours." And so saying, or rather singing, they unwrapped the army blanket and revealed an ordinary baby, quite like Mary's own, except that he was very white.

"Oh, he's beautiful," Mary said politely. "And I'd like to oblige you, but I'm not so sure my husband would be pleased."

"She will never know the difference."

"She's got a very sharp eye."

"There is no alternative. It is destiny."

"I see," Mary muttered, wondering how she might exact some advantage from destiny before yielding to it. "Still and all . . . what would you do with him if I let you have him?"

"Raise him as my very own, of course. And then when he grows up he will have eternal youth and give his life to love."

"You mean he'll be a movie star?"

"That is very possible."

Mary was impressed in spite of herself. But only for a moment.

"Well, I was hoping my son would be president of a large corporation. I don't like the idea—"

"But, Mary," said the fairies, "you can make my son into a businessman."

Mary pretended not to have heard. She said, "Movie stars are very rich, aren't they? And here I am the poorest of the very poor."

The fairies were growing impatient. They shrugged

their slender shoulders, rose into the air and came down firmly on their toes. "You are wasting my time," they said loudly. "And you are standing in the way of destiny."

Although so shamed by their reproach that she flushed hotly, Mary wasn't yet ready to surrender. "And what about your baby? He'll have those wings, like yours. And on top of being poor, I'll have a son who'll be the laughingstock of the neighborhood. I deserve compensation for that kind of humiliation."

"No, he will not have wings. A fairy child that suckles mortal's milk never grows wings."

As the fairies then started toward Baby's basket, Mary sprang past them and grabbed the sleeping infant up in her arms. "How much?" she screamed. "How much?"

No sooner had Mary uttered these words than the two fairies opened like a fan. They became a dozen fairies and these opened, becoming a hundred and then perhaps a thousand fairies. The room was stuffed full of them, from wall to wall, from floor to ceiling. Mary took a sharp breath and fairies flew into her nose and throat. She spit some out of her mouth. They were soon in her ears and under her apron. And their faces no longer seemed beautiful but ugly; they had long pointed eye-teeth like vampires, and the very sight of them pierced Mary's eyes and even her heart. They weren't good at all, Mary thought, they were evil, abominable, and probably they were completely naked. Probably their gowns were just an optical illusion.

"Give me that child," the multitude sang in their one pure lyrical voice.

While poor Mary stood there helpless, they tore Baby out of her frail arms. She closed her eyes and cried and stamped her feet and shrieked at the top of her lungs—until she heard that whirring sound again. Then, just very slightly, she opened her eyes and saw the fairies flying through the window, out into the courtyard, and up to the sky.

"Good riddance," she yelled, and when the last ones had gone, slammed the window shut.

In the basket where her own little boy had so recently lain there was now the pale fairy child. Mary felt disgusted and wondered whether he was good or bad. He was definitely naked. He didn't look as though he could ever be president of a large corporation, or anything else. And what would Emily think of all this? After frowning at him for a minute or two, Mary lifted the baby out of the cradle and put him to her breast to give him suck. It would be better in any case if he didn't grow wings.

11

Little Luis opened the door and after a stunned silence screamed, "A cuckoo man is here. A cuckoo man is here."

Ismael was in the back room having a nightmare about being trapped in someone else's dream. It was sticky and moist. He shouted, hoping to wake the sleeper, but his voice oozed soundlessly like glue in the dark shapeless dream. Kicking was no good either, for his feet either stuck or else hit without impact as if under water.

When Luis screamed, Ismael woke and knew at once that it was Tommy. He sprang off the bed and raced through the apartment in his underwear, a red nylon posing strap. Halfway across the kitchen he realized he had an erection. Grabbing a dish towel he continued running.

All the kids and Mama were now standing at the door, and everyone was silent except little Luis who sobbed and hiccuped with his face pressed against Mama's belly. Tommy was trying to speak but nothing came out of his lopsided mouth. He had the collar of his raincoat high around his neck and the brim of his hat low over his forehead. Nonetheless you could see his face.

"Hey, Tommy-boy, glad to see you."

Mama and the children seemed incredulous that Ismael should know this man. Holding the towel in front of himself with one hand, he pulled Tommy through the doorway with the other. He led him across the apartment to the back room and shut the door after them.

"It sure is good to see you, Tommy. I was just dreaming about you. We were in Central Park and it was Easter. I know it was Easter because there were colored eggs—"

"What are you holding that towel in front of you for? Afraid of something?"

"The towel? Oh, I didn't have—my family was . . . I better put my pants on."

"No, don't."

"All right." Ismael shrugged as though it didn't matter. But it did, because although his erection was gone, everything had folded wrong, and his basket looked enormous. Even tempting. "There's that damn mosquito," he cried and leaped across the room. He pretended to kill a mosquito, and while his back was turned to Tommy, adjusted the posing strap, feeling a little uneasy about his bare behind. "It kept buzzing in my ear before—what are you shaking your head about, Tommy?"

"Nothing," he said slowly.

"Well, then, why don't you sit down?"

Tommy looked around the room and Ismael felt ashamed of the linoleum and the five beds.

"I guess you were never here before," he said. "Well, come on, pull up a bed then, and sit down."

"It's been two weeks," Tommy said without moving.

"What has?"

"Since I saw you."

"Two weeks! It couldn't be. My God, has it really been that long? No, it couldn't be. I have just been so exhausted, Tommy, you can't imagine. It has been murder! You'd think I had the plague or something. Or B.O. or something. I look look look all day for work and no one wants to hire me."

He thought Tommy smiled ironically, but of course it was impossible to really tell. Maybe he was scowling. In any case, there was no mistaking what happened next: Tommy flung open his raincoat and dropped his pants. He did it with such speed and such dash that Ismael gaped in admiration.

"Have you gone out of your mind?" said Ismael, recovering. He glanced at the door, then went and hung the dish towel over the knob in order to cover the keyhole. *"Please,* Tommy. The kids could walk in at any minute." He leaned against the door, just in case.

"Look!" Tommy said, lifting his genitals. "Aren't these still beautiful? Look at your old friend Huck hanging his sad head. Isn't he still cute?"

"He's as cute as can be, Tommy, and you're all beautiful altogether. Just please get your pants up before somebody walks in on us."

"I don't care who walks in."

"Then you don't care about me. You're selfish, and you were always selfish. All you ever did think about was yourself, even when you sent me to Puerto Rico. You were just thinking about yourself—not about me or how I'd feel."

"How you'd feel! The only feeling you're capable of is greed."

"Then what do you want me for?"

"I like the way your shit tastes."

He pulled his pants up clumsily and unglamorously.

They sat down, but on different beds, and there was a very long silence. Ismael was obliged to break it first, hating Tommy for being able to sit concealed behind his ugliness. He said, "I guess you never have been here before, have you? Tell me which one of my pictures you like best." Three or four dozen photographs of himself were pasted up on the wall.

"That's a very good idea," Tommy said dryly. "Papering the room with your face."

"I'm not doing anything of the sort. I know you—all you want to do is humiliate me, that's all." He waited,

48

and again he had to break the silence. "Well, which picture do you like best?"

"That one." Tommy pointed to the big plaster crucifix that had a yellow wax rose at its base. "I like that one best," he said softly.

Ismael smiled and flushed, then crossed and uncrossed his legs. "That's sacrilege, Tommy."

"I'm not a Catholic. I'm an Ismaelite."

Ismael smiled vaguely and glanced around the room, for he feared he was missing the point. There was another extremely long silence. "How are you getting on with your shrink?" he asked, somewhat irritated.

"I've stopped going."

"Now, why'd you ever do that?"

"I can't afford him any more. Besides, he admitted candidly that he couldn't analyze me out of my face. Will you come home with me now, Ismael, or is it the sheerest folly and most utter madness to ask?"

Ismael stamped his foot. "No, it isn't the utterest—oh, you are so damn selfish! Here I am in bed asleep at ten o'clock in the evening because I've been out looking for a job all day. My feet are worn down to the bone. You don't ever think of me, ever. Just because you've always had money, you can spend all your time thinking about yourself. And I can't come tonight. I'll come tomorrow."

"That's what you said two weeks ago."

"It wasn't two weeks ago in the first place. It was four or five days ago. Now, don't start getting me really mad, Tommy, I'm warning you."

Another silence.

"I have to go to sleep," said Ismael. "I can hardly keep my eyes open."

To his surprise, Tommy stood up. Ismael went to the door and put his hand on the knob, but waited for Tommy who was walking slowly toward him.

They faced each other without smiling.

"Let me give Moby Dick a little kiss, baby," Tommy said hoarsely and fell to his knees.

"For Christ's sake!" Ismael hissed, pulling his posing strap up.

They struggled briefly.

"One tiny little kiss and I'll go."

Ismael clicked his tongue, then raised his eyes to the ceiling so as not to have to watch what was happening. He sighed twice, the second time in spite of himself. It was exciting with Mama and the kids just on the other side of the door.

Later, when Ismael was dressing to go out, he thought with sudden anger how Tommy had pressed a ten-dollar bill into his hand as they said goodbye. The nerve! He really had some nerve! Ismael tore off his posing strap and began furiously tugging on his gunmetal pants.

12

Dear Dr. Franzblau,

I am going out of my mind. Sometimes I think of killing myself, that's how tormented I am. There is no one I can talk to. I have no friends. The one person in the world who was my friend has now become the person I am trying to escape from. Please please tell me what to do.

It all began two years ago this month on my graduation day from Junior High. I was sixteen then. Maybe that sounds a little old to be getting out of Junior High, but I didn't come to the States until I was ten. I'm not dumb. Or wild. I graduated fifth in the class and won a few prizes. In poetry and something else. Maybe sewing or drawing. I can't even remember now. Those things used to seem so important to me, but now all that is just trivia.

I was, and still am to be frank, a very pretty girl of cafe-au-lait color, and boys were always after me. I never paid any attention to them, partly because they were so rough and I was afraid of them, but mainly because I lived in a world of dreams and pretty things. I was *completely* innocent. I mean, I sort of knew the facts of life, but not too clearly. I had no friends except my beloved mother.

Anyway, I wore a yellow chiffon dress to graduation and a yellow rose in my hair which isn't kinky. I knew I looked very attractive. After the services a few girls who had never been too friendly to me before asked me to take a walk with them. I thought, what the hell, why not, though I didn't like them much. They were rather vulgar and I knew they were coming on just because I won a few prizes. But I thought, why not?

When we got around to Times Square an American boy on a motorcycle started following me. I knew he was following ME, but of course the others all thought he was following all of us. You know how girls are. Stupid and conceited.

The boy tried talking to me a few times but I ignored him. Also because he was dressed entirely in black leather like some kind of freaky cop. Pants, jacket, helmet and gloves. Only his white silk scarf wasn't black leather. Or his socks, naturally. His face wasn't bad. In fact, he was really very handsome. He kept asking me if I wanted a ride on his motorcycle. The girls all said,

"Better not, Isobel," and giggled. I knew they were jealous because he wasn't asking them, so just out of spite I agreed to go for a short ride. Besides, I noticed that he wasn't really a boy. I mean, as it turned out he was twenty-seven. And I've always had a big thing for older men like teachers and presidents, not that twenty-seven is old. Older than myself.

I had to put my arms around him to stay on the motorcycle and he kept pushing my hands under his jacket. He wasn't wearing a shirt. His skin felt nice but naturally I made a fuss about it. We went for a long long ride, down to the Battery where we took the ferry and watched the sun set and the lights come on, and then up to the East Seventies, to the fancy part.

He said, "This is where I live. How about coming in for a drink or a smoke?"

I acted bored so as not to show how excited I was. I'm just a simple Puerto Rican after all and I never expected to see the insides of a place like that, except maybe as a maid. Besides I thought for sure his family was in there with him. At that time I didn't know that Americans left home practically as soon as they could walk.

Someone like you, a doctor with a newspaper column and all is probably used to the kind of place over on the East Side. But I wasn't. You know, carpets, drapes, chandeliers. Pretty doodads that cost an arm and a leg wherever you looked. I went for it in a big way. When I looked in the mirror over the fireplace my face turned into a mixture of Liz Taylor and Jackie Kennedy. Teddibly glaborous, as Tommy would say. The thing I liked best was a spiral staircase made of ebony wood in one corner of the room. Each stair had a rectangle of stuffed ruby velvet framed by brass. I didn't know then that that was the stairway leading to my destruction.

I suppose I had about six martinis, or rather Gibsons, and also smoked a couple of joints. I'd never had a martini before, that's how innocent I was, or for that matter smoked. And I didn't know you weren't supposed to mix pot and alcohol. Tommy knew, but of course he was busy seducing me, which I had no idea he was doing. I mean, I kept imagining his mother was somewhere around and probably a few dozen servants. So I drank and smoked, drank and smoked. And laughed. He was a scream! Witty, intelligent and a real person. Not just a wise guy or a hood. I really liked him a lot.

After a couple of hours he said, "I bet you a dollar you can't find the bed." I was dying to take a walk up that stairway anyhow, so I got up and headed for it. He had to stay behind me to keep me from falling. I loved the way my feet felt landing on the ruby velvet. I didn't have my shoes on. The stairway led right into the bedroom. He had a lot of dumbbells and athletic equipment which is how he managed to keep such a good physique. The bed was a four-poster with an embroidered canopy, simply gorgeous. It came from Fez—a city in Morocco.

Tommy said, "All right, you win. Here's your dollar. You want to try for two?"

I said, "Two what?"

He said, "I bet you two dollars I can get my clothes off faster than you."

So that is how Tommy and I met and fell in love with each other.

That was two years, two long long years ago. I used to visit him every night after work. His work, not mine. He worked for Time-Life Inc, and earned a fortune. I didn't do any work. I'm ashamed to admit this, but I want to be honest with you, Dr. Franzblau, and I hope you won't put me down for it. It was Tommy's fault anyhow. He said he didn't believe women should work. But that wasn't the real reason. The real reason was he was madly in love with me and insanely jealous. People talk about Latin passion, but let me tell you, there's nothing like an anglosaxon for a dirty mind.

Anyhow, my family is very poor. Papa is dead and Mama struggles along with six kids on welfare. So I had to take money from Tommy because Mama expected me to go to work after Junior High. And he wouldn't let me. I really wanted to go to work. I sort of thought I could maybe work in a theater or in fashion. After I met Tommy I thought I'd like to learn about interior decorating. But he wouldn't hear of it. I told Mama I was working nights in a factory. Long hours short pay. I brought home between thirty and forty a week, after taxes, meaning a little for myself. With the welfare this added up to a lot.

Sometimes we went away to the country or the shore for the weekend, for swimming or hiking or skiing.

Sometimes even for parachuting out of airplanes. He was mad about that. I didn't like it too much. I used to sit and wait and help drag him out of that laundry bag. Now and then we went to visit Tommy's broad-minded friends for a couple of days. I was ashamed at first because we weren't married and not of the same race. Though I'm not black. I am cafe-au-lait. His friends were tolerant. They talked about the theater and pot and hallucinogens constantly. I wasn't too crazy about them as they were always trying to be natural and easy and free. Hip. It got on my nerves, but they were really all right. There were three or four different couples altogether. The reason we stopped going to them was because Tommy was jealous. He imagined I was doing things with everyone. We had violent fights over this and finally just stayed home. I didn't mind. He taught me a lot of things. He educated me more than my Junior High did. And we loved each other in spite of constant fights. Basically we were happy and extremely compatible, especially in sexual relations.

This kind of life went on until six months ago. Then for a few days he sat around very depressed and melancholy. He used to do this a lot. It usually meant he'd uncovered something at the shrink's, usually something pretty disgusting which he'd forget about in a day or two. But this time his mood went on and on and on. And he didn't pick on me the way he did with his insights, to make me suffer over the bad secret feelings he had about me or whatever bullshit he found out at the shrink. Oh, excuse me, Dr. Franzblau, that sounds terrible. I mean, I myself often considered going to an analyst. But I don't think Tommy's doctor was too good.

Anyway, I was beginning to feel maybe he was tired of me, though on the other hand he did a lot of hugging and kissing and crying. I never asked what the matter was. I'm not that kind of person. I know I'll find out when the time comes. Anyway, one night out of the clear blue he pulled a one-way ticket to San Juan out of his pocket and said, "How would you like to fly to Puerto Rico for a couple of weeks?"

I said, "Love to, but you already took your vacation last summer. Can you take some more?"

"Not me. Just you. You go alone. I thought you might enjoy the trip. It's your homeland, after all. I have a little extra money now because of my Christmas bonus."

Oh. Oh no. Oh ho ho ho no sirree sir. You're not going to dump Isobel just like that. I didn't say that of course. What I said was, "I can't live without you, Tommy, even for just a couple of weeks." I meant it too. I loved him very much, more than anyone on earth except Mama and the kids.

This conversation ended in a violent fight. We both cried and he swore he loved me. He said he couldn't tell me why he was asking me to go, but that I should trust him. There was no other woman or anything like that, and he said if he was insincere he would obviously make up some cover story. Which made sense.

So I went. I stayed with my aunt and uncle near San Juan and it was fun for a few weeks. I met a lot of people and did the town a lot. Tommy sent me ten dollars

every week. The rest of my salary he sent by money order to Mama. His letters were funny right from the beginning. Short and hysterical. Full of crazy poetry and
dirty words. Love love love. But he didn't say anything
about me coming back.

This went on for nearly four months. Every time I
wrote please send me a ticket, I want to go home, he
wrote back, stay a little longer, the weather is terrible—
or something like that.

Finally I wrote and said I was sick and tired of San
Juan and the boring scene there, that I hated having to
go to bars, drink and flirt, and that if he didn't send me a
ticket by return mail, I'd get the money together myself
somehow, and not to blame me. The ticket came a few
days later.

He didn't meet me at Kennedy. There were a lot of
Puerto Ricans on the plane and I thought I'd wait until
they see me stepping down the gangway being met by
this handsome ritzy American. But he wasn't there, and
he certainly knew which flight I was coming on as I'd
sent him a wire.

I took a taxi into town, straight to Tommy's place. I
had the keys naturally. The light was on in the living
room. I could see that from the street. I dragged my
bags up the steps. You know how cab drivers are. Anyway, I unlocked the door exhausted, so I wasn't sure at
first I was seeing right. Tommy was sitting in a chair
under the floor lamp with all the light shining on his
face. Like a stage set. He'd prepared it. He was sitting
there waiting for me to look at him. I thought at first he

was wearing a mask, except it moved. I can't really describe his face, Dr. Franzblau. It was all sort of pulled around to one side, but it didn't always stay there. It dropped sometimes. It slid around here and there like it was alive or something. I stood there unable to believe my eyes. My handsome winsome Tommy!

I couldn't open my mouth. I just stood there. Finally he said, "Welcome home, lover, want a drink?" He got up and poured some whiskey out for both of us. I needed it badly. "How was your trip, have a good time in those San Juan bars? Get fucked a lot?" Excuse me, Dr. Franzblau, for repeating such things. You see what a state I'm in.

I still couldn't open my mouth. But he went on talking. "What's the matter, forget how to hablar yinglis after being with the spicks so long? Wow, I can smell foreskin right across the room. Come on, baby, yack." He said stuff like that.

Finally I managed to speak. I said, "Tommy, Tommy, what happened to you?"

"What happened to me? When? I don't know what you mean. Oh, you mean the old pussy puss? Don't you like it better this way? I had my face lifted—I mean, shifted. Lowered, raised, cranked around. It's all the rage in New York these days. Want yours done? Come on, baby, how's about a kiss right in the old kisser?"

But he didn't try to kiss me or anything. We just sat drinking. He had to sit right under the lamp out of some kind of poisonous spite. Then he asked me about Puerto Rico but I didn't have anything to say.

I said, "How's your job?"

"Job? Oh, I quit of course. What would a face like mine do among all those beautiful people?"

"Tommy, when did this happen? How did it happen? Why didn't you write me about it?"

"Oh, well, baby, there didn't seem much point. I had this tiny little tumor see, and the doctors said there was a chance if they operated that it might turn out this way. I'm in great shape now, though. Look, no tumors!"

"So that was why you sent me away!"

He didn't trust me. He had never trusted me. I really hated him when I realized that. If only he hadn't sent me away, things might have been *so* different. If only he had told me the truth and let me go through it with him. But he acted like I was some common prostitute or something. Then to make matters worse, he said, "I bet you a dollar you can't find the bed. Or I guess I better bet you fifty dollars now. Or maybe a hundred."

And I was practically his wife!

I got very mad, but I swallowed it. Not just that once but a lot of times afterwards. He left the bedlamp on out of spite. Even when his face was nice he never left that light on. He was always arranging candles and special colored lights and fancy effects. Never plain white naked light. Except now. I mean, he wasn't going to let me lose sight of that face for a minute. But I went through with it. I've got a lot of guts. You have to have to get along in this world.

When it was over, he hugged me a lot and cried. He kept saying God was good and that I was good. Then he talked about his operation and how much he loved me and was afraid to let me see him and that after all it was a mistake to have mistrusted me. Could I ever forgive him? I just wished I could drop dead.

I can't tell you what my life has been like since then. What can I do, my feelings have really changed. And it isn't my fault. I admit it has a lot to do with the way he looks now. But it has more to do with his not trusting me and the whole shock and everything. I really want to break up with him, but I don't have the nerve because I still care about him deeply. I've tried to stop going over to his place, but he comes around here to my house every night now. Mama tells him I'm not home, but he waits out in the street till dawn. I can see him from the window, pacing and pacing. I can't go up to him and say I don't love you any more, your face and your character disgust me, leave me alone. I'm afraid he might kill himself or kill me. I am in hiding, Dr. Franzblau, in hiding.

Please tell me what to do. I implore you.

Sincerest regards from your devoted and admiring reader. Please excuse the length of this letter.

Yours truly,
(Miss) Isobel Rosa

P.S. If you write about me in your column, don't even mention my initials. Tommy and I used to read your column aloud to each other now and then. He might still read it, though I doubt it. You could refer to me as Yellow Rose.

13

Tomtom Jim sat in a clearing, under the stars, blowing a merry tune on his Pan's pipe. He was a black man who had been sent by God to murder all the human beings he could lay his hands on and feed them to the beasts. Drawn by his music, animals had come to him from all corners of the world and they lived in peace together. As once they had taken refuge in Noah's ark, they now came to Tomtom Jim's forest where antelope and lion, wolf and peacock lived in friendship and peace. Here they lay together, listened and dozed together, dreamed and laughed together, and together tore people to pieces. Midst this harmony there was but one discord, which was that Tomtom Jim longed for a human mate.

Yet, if in his heart he was sad, the animals never knew of it, for he kept his sorrow hidden.

A silver fox which had been sleeping with its head on Tomtom Jim's thigh now stood up on its hind legs and sang a lament about man's conquest of nature. The last part of the song, however, was joyful, since it told of the coming of Tomtom Jim and how single-handed he would bring innocence back to the world.

"Amen!" the animals chanted as the silver fox took her bows.

"Amen!" said Tomtom Jim though he didn't feel entirely innocent.

Suddenly, from the forest, there came a noise. It was a human noise, but it was unusual. All the animals grew tense. Ears sprang up; feathers and fur stiffened; tails shot out. Tomtom Jim put down his pipe and listened nervously.

"Don't be scared," he whispered. But the noise came closer and the beasts began to smell of panic. "Don't be scared," Tomtom Jim reassured them. "It's just your supper on its way."

The sound was almost upon them.

All at once and silently, the animals slipped from the clearing and fled in among the trees to the north. Tomtom Jim lifted himself to a squatting position, from which he could leap. He put his pipe in his pocket now and took out a switchblade knife. Snapping the knife open, he covered the gleaming blade with his fingers so as not to give his position away.

The human sound became clearer: it was the sound of tears.

Presently a thin girl with a child in her arms walked into the clearing. It wasn't the child who was crying. Wrapped in an old army blanket, the infant had his big dry eyes wide open and a toothy grin on his face. Tomtom Jim's first holy impulse was to kill them both and feed them to his friends, but he hesitated, for he had never seen such a pair in his forest and he wondered about them.

"Stop!" he shouted. "Don't come any closer. What do you want?"

Behind him, in the trees, the hungry frightened animals waited anxiously for the kill.

Because of her grief, Mary Poorpoor had no fear. "I'm looking for my son," she said.

"What's that you have there?"

"A changeling."

Tomtom Jim didn't know what a changeling was, but he was too proud to admit this.

"That's no changeling," he said.

"Yes he is. Honestly."

"I don't believe you."

"Why would I lie?"

"Because you're human. If you don't tell me the truth, I'll kill you." He took his hand off the blade and flashed it around to show Mary he was serious.

"That *is* the truth. The fairies took my own son away and left me theirs, and my husband abandoned me because of it. I have been looking and searching in every corner of the world for the kingdom of the fairies. I was told it might be here."

"Who told you that?"

"A little brown dog I met at the edge of the woods. He was very hungry and I let him suckle at my breast. I have plenty of milk." Mary opened her blouse to show Tomtom Jim how full her tits were.

Tomtom Jim's heart was softened by the girl. She seemed almost as innocent and harmless as a wild animal. Closing his knife, he stood up and went to her.

"Why don't you stay here and live with me?" he said. "There's lots of food and we could have fun together."

"I couldn't do that. I must find my little boy. But I greatly appreciate your offer."

Tomtom Jim couldn't take his eyes off Mary's pretty little bosom. He said, "This changeling has a very nasty face. The nastiest I've ever seen on a changeling. Look at those big eye teeth, will you? Let's kill him."

"No. Oh no no. That would be heartless. Besides, if this one is killed, the fairies might never give me back my own son."

Tomtom Jim reflected for a moment. "I tell you what," he said. "I know the world better than any other man. If you want I'll go with you and together we'll look for your little boy."

"Thank you, thank you," said Mary, throwing her free arm around him and sobbing so loudly that he didn't hear the mournful wailing of the beasts behind him.

14

Alone except for the sharp-toothed changeling, hungry and homeless, desperate, Mary Poorpoor wandered for many months through the cold indifferent city. One bright morning she found herself outside a small park and, not knowing it was forbidden to the general public, she pushed open the iron gate and walked in.

Could this at last be fairyland, she wondered, feeling faint from the beauty of the place. It was the prettiest garden she had ever seen, all laid out with narrow secret paths that wound between high bushes and beds of flowers and tall gracefully trimmed trees. And the people too were pretty, though they seemed perhaps fatter than other fairies she had known.

A woman went by wheeling a baby carriage the size of a small car. Strange, thought Mary. And then it happened again. And still again.

They must have enormous babies here, Mary told herself and decided that if she passed another such carriage she would peer inside. She walked on. A few minutes later, when she had stopped to smell some roses, a middle-aged woman dressed like a nurse came down the path pushing a carriage. Mary stood on her toes as the nurse went by, and to her astonishment she saw no baby.

"Cute, isn't he?" said the woman noticing Mary's interest.

"Adorable," said Mary.

Nurse and carriage disappeared round a bend in the path.

While Mary stood puzzling this over, a man in uniform touched her shoulder and asked if she had a key. Of course, Mary had no key to anywhere.

"I'm afraid, madam," the man said, "that you will have to leave the park as it is forbidden to the general public. It is only for persons who have the key."

Mary hated the man. "This is a free country," she told him. "Don't you know that? I can go anywhere I please."

"I beg your pardon?" the man asked vaguely. He was distracted because Baby's blanket had fallen open and his genitals were hanging down below his shirt. They were remarkably large for his age.

"I said, this is a free country," Mary repeated.

"Yes, it is," the man agreed and without further ado took Mary Poorpoor by the arm and started pulling her out of the garden. Mary burst into tears.

"Just one minute, Johnson," a lady called. "What's going on here." She wasn't wheeling a baby carriage.

"Nothing to worry about, Miss Emily," said the man in uniform.

"That's for me to decide, Johnson, isn't it?" the lady said kindly but firmly, and then turned to Mary Poorpoor. "Hello, my lovely girl, are you having trouble?"

"I don't have the key," Mary told her.

Miss Emily smiled. "That's a very pretty baby. I'll bet it's a boy, isn't it?" she said, tickling Baby's balls. "What's his name?"

Mary liked the kind lady very much indeed, although she was odd. For example, her hair had been cut so short that she was practically bald, and her mustache hairs were darkened with eyebrow pencil. And she wore a severely tailored tweed suit. But Mary liked the lady, so in order to make her happy, and since the baby had no name anyhow, she said, "His name is Emilio."

Miss Emily put her hands on her hips, threw back her head and roared with laughter. "Well, that's a coincidence! Because my name is Emily."

"Pleased to meet you. My name is Mary," said the little mother with a respectful curtsy.

"Where do you live, pretty Mary?"

"Nowhere. Just nowhere!" The tears began rolling down her cheeks again, and as they dropped off her jaw, Emilio caught them in his mouth and grinned. "I'm all alone in the world and homeless."

"You poor darling. Dry your tears. Now, now, child, you're not alone or homeless any more."

15

James Madison lay on the cot eating chocolates out of a heart-shaped box. He knew they would do something awful to him like make his urine red or turn the flood-lights on in his head or make him vomit, but he ate them anyhow, since he was under orders and besides they tasted good.

In his rectum, which wasn't yet spacious enough, were five frankfurters tied in a bundle. Later, John Doe had warned him, he would have to practice with a hu-man head and after that a crystal chandelier, a bathtub, and finally a station wagon. Then perhaps he would be ready. Perhaps.

The floor was littered with wads of crumpled pink and pale-blue toilet paper which, in the candlelight, looked like flowers growing out of the wood. The room was like a strange interior garden. Also on the floor were countless magazines and comic books, gifts from John Doe. Occasionally James Madison reached over and picked one up, flipped through it, then dropped it with his arm extended so that it made a wind through the flowers and caused the candles to flicker.

In one of the magazines he now came across a photograph of Manhattan at night. His breast swelled with longing and homesickness. The picture rode off the page and came to rest in the middle of the room, miniature but sparkling and glamorous, charged with life. The slender buildings were made of jewels. Lights blazed. All the noises of the city sounded in his ears.

"Oh, Magic City," he cried.

16

Yesterday he was Mary Queen of Scots. The day before that he'd been Joan of Arc, and his brassiere and panties had melted into hard black crumbs that stuck painfully to his body. He'd had to pick them out of the hair like a monkey. Earlier in the week he'd been St. Catherine, and he was still troubled by a slight lumbago. He'd also been Edward II, stamped to death while suffering a redhot poker up the ass. He'd been a Crusader drawn and quartered by an Arab, a seventeenth-century Englishwoman hanged for stealing a loaf of bread, an ancient Hebrew stoned for knowing carnally a tiger. He wondered if anything nice had ever happened. Or was history just a list of tortures?

Who was he today? He didn't know, and it worried him. He was in a cold stone cell again, like yesterday's tower, but this time there were great flaming tapers. For a moment he believed he was a Negro in a Klansman's cellar, then a Christian about to be fed to the lions. He was on his knees, waiting and wishing he knew who he was. Anything was better than this vagueness.

John Doe handed him a sheet of paper. "Learn this by heart and repeat it aloud on your knees six times a day at intervals of at least two hours. Whenever I enter this room, the first thing you do is get on your knees and recite it. If I fail to appear for twenty-four hours, begin reciting the prayer every fifteen minutes night and day until I do appear. In any case, whatever the circumstances, you're to draw blood after each prayer. A real cut, not just a superficial scratch. Use a razor blade. That's more exciting than a knife. Anywhere on your body. I will tabulate the number of scratches every time I see you. You can begin now."

James Madison mumbled, "I don't know it by heart." He was terribly disturbed because if he didn't know who he was, how could he know when to apply this rule or any rule?

"You're allowed to read it. But just this once."

James Madison pulled a miserable face.

"What's the matter now?"

"I don't know who I am or who you are. I mean, who am I supposed to be?"

"What difference does it make?"

"I have to know because I don't like the way it feels not knowing. Who am I?"

"You're James Madison."

"How can I be James Madison if I'm in some cold wet prison with flaming tapers all around?"

"Well, that's how it is."

"That isn't fair."

John Doe was outraged. "What do you mean, it isn't fair? Have you gone crazy or something?"

"That's who I really am: James Madison. And I'm in a room on the fifth floor of a tenement on Madison Street. You're getting me all mixed up." He was so upset that he started up off his knees.

"Get down there, you cocksucker!" John Doe whipped his belt off and doubled it over. "Don't think! Just obey! Start reading!"

" 'In your dream is my only awakening. In your fantasy is my only reality. In my hell is your only heaven. In your moment is my only eternity. In your devil is my only God. In my death is your only birth. In your destruction is my—' "

" 'In *my* destruction,' " John Doe corrected.

He studied the page. "Oh. I see. 'In *my* destruction is your only creation. Come to me, murderer. Come to me, murderer.' I don't understand a word of it, except those last lines. My brassiere and panties are gone, burned to a crisp when I was Joan of Arc. I don't know who I am."

John Doe sighed. "I'll get you some new things tomorrow. Don't nag me. Repeat those last two lines again."

"You mean, 'Come to me, murderer. Come to me, murderer'?"

"Yes. I think it would be more diverting if you said them a dozen time rather than just twice."

"All right."

While he repeated the lines, John Doe went into the kitchen and came back with a razor blade. "Here," he said.

James Madison examined himself and then, closing his eyes, made a slit over his left nipple. A line of blood appeared among the hairs and slowly dripped down his chest. He still felt rather miserable but thought it wiser not to pursue matters. He folded the sheet of paper carefully into four and dropped the blade inside. When he looked up, John Doe had the belt raised again.

"Strip!" he said harshly.

Today was a very strange day indeed. "But I haven't a stitch on. How can I strip? For God's sake, who am I supposed to be?"

"I'll flay you alive!"

The belt came down fast and hard across his thighs, and James Madison screamed more loudly than he ever had before. The scream clanged around the cell like chains. John Doe stood very still, his eyes motionless. He was listening. Long after there was no sound, he stood listening. Then he walked on tiptoe across the stone floor and put his ear to the door. Outside, the world was silent.

He said, "Don't you ever scream like that again. Or the game's over."

James Madison began trembling. "I'm awfully sorry. It just slipped out." And hoping to make amends, he added, "It's just that I liked it so much."

"Oh, you did, did you?" The tone of menace in his voice was hollow, forced. He went to the bridge table and mixed himself a drink. "Tell me. Do you think about me a lot when I'm not here?"

James Madison didn't know what answer was expected. After hesitating, he said, "How do you mean?"

"Do you think about me and get hot?"

Now he knew. "Yes, terribly. All the time."

John Doe began pacing back and forth while he put his belt on.

"I've got to go. I've got to go," he muttered.

James Madison went cold. "Where?" he whispered.

Clutching his basket, John Doe smiled and minced over to James Madison. "Would you like to touch it?"

"You know I would."

"You've never touched it, have you? You've never even seen it. Have you? Maybe I'll go away now and I won't come back and then you'll never ever get a chance to see it. How would you like that?"

James Madison lowered his eyes. He was too pained to reply.

"Would you give your life to see it, touch it, suck it?"

"Happily, gratefully."

"Do you imagine it when I'm not here and jerk off thinking about it?"

"Yes, yes. Oh, yes, yes, yes. Come to me, murderer."

John Doe laughed. "Close your eyes and open your mouth. Would you eat my shit?"

"I already have."

"I said mouth open. How do you know it was really mine?"

Mouth open, eyes shut, James Madison waited. He heard tiptoeing. He heard the door. He was alone again. Now he knew who he was.

He got up off his knees and lay down on the cot, opening the box of chocolates.

17

DEAR ISMAEL,

It is now a month since I last saw you, and I can no longer deceive myself into imagining that there is anything left between us, nor any hope, nor any possibility. I have loved you more than life itself.

I am going away—where, I don't know. I have sold my furniture and motorcycle. The enclosed check is for all the money I have in the world. I hope it can make you happy and give your charming family some rest from worldly woes, at least temporarily.

May God bless you always, and keep you always in His care.

With, at least, a love that has not changed, I am forever your

TOMMY

18

Three in the morning on the East River Drive. The Jaguar convertible swam through the damp heavy night like a silver canoe. Ismael looked dazed, or maybe blind, but he handled the car well.

He parked on East Seventy-third Street, under a tree. Tommy's windows were dark and curtainless, abandoned.

"Do you want to do it here?" asked his companion, a young blond with large ears who claimed to be an English nobleman.

Ismael said nothing.

"I'd like it here. Would it be terribly dangerous?" he asked, but Ismael wasn't even looking at him. The nobleman became impatient. "You've driven around for hours and now you won't talk to me. I'm tired of this. What sort of Arab are you anyhow? I thought you were going to fuck me."

His eyes fixed on Tommy's windows, Ismael suddenly bellowed: "Tommy, Tommy where have you gone?"

"You're really too much. Do you want the fuzz all over us?" He'd suspected Ismael was bad news from the beginning, which was why he'd liked him. But he didn't want trouble with the police.

"Tommy, Tommy, I'll never love anybody like I loved you."

The nobleman took a tube of codeine from his pocket and dropped all the pills down his throat. Now, at least, he'd be able to get to sleep without feeling frustrated.

"See you," he said, getting out of the car. He slammed the door with his hip.

Leaning his head down on the steering wheel, Ismael burst into heartbroken sobs. "What have I done with my life?" he wailed.

19

Death held no surprises, except that he was handsomer than Xavier had imagined. He had a thin white face and very thin white hands, and his dark eyes were not unfriendly. He wore black robes that hid his feet and a black hood. With a preoccupied look, like a meditating monk, he strolled through the garden in the moonlight, stopping now and then at the flowers. Once or twice he bent to examine them more closely, but he touched nothing. When he saw the roses, he smiled.

If he had noticed Xavier, who was sitting in the grass under the dark windows of his room, he had in no way shown it.

Xavier stood up and went to the rose bush where he

broke off a full young rose. He pricked his finger on a thorn.

"Ouch," he said, and Death, who was standing over the irises, turned. Xavier extended his arm. They walked toward each other, smiling.

"This is for you," Xavier said.

When he laid the rose on Death's outstretched hand, a drop of blood fell from his finger onto the white un-lined palm. The drop of blood lay beside the flower like a small dark jewel.

"I'm not trying to bribe you," Xavier said.

"I know that." His voice was flat but otherwise unre-markable. "Thank you."

They began strolling together through the garden.

"That's a wild cherry tree, isn't it?" asked Death.

"Yes. I planted it myself when I was a little boy. I mean, I threw a lot of pits around the garden. This one grew. I'm not afraid of you."

"That's good. I'm not afraid of you either."

Xavier wondered if Death was pulling his leg. "Shall I tell you why I'm not afraid of you?"

Death nodded, looking him in the eyes.

"Because you seem very old-fashioned. And also, you look like a Jew."

Death laughed. He had a pleasant, easy laugh, like a man without worries.

They went around back of the house and stopped at the snowball tree.

"I've never been inside this house before," Death said.

"Really? That's odd. It's a very old house, nearly a century, I think. And we've only lived here twenty years or so."

"I know. But people always moved out before they died."

"Until now."

Death didn't acknowledge Xavier's comment. He said, "Forty or fifty years ago there was an old drunk who lived here. Every so often he'd fall down off the porch and break his head open on the walk. You may have heard about him from the neighbors."

"I never talk to the neighbors," said Xavier.

"Finally he died of TB. But in a hospital. I wish people wouldn't die in hospitals, though of course it's none of my business. If I were human, I'd go out to a garden or a wood to die. I loathe going to hospitals; they're so sinister. And the more elegant they are, the more sinister. I often wish I didn't have to go there."

"Well, why do you go there then?"

"I have no choice either." They continued walking, and Death lifted the rose to his face. "Mmm, delicious. You do have a marvelous garden here. It's the nicest on the whole street."

"It's for you," Xavier said warmly, as if offering a bouquet.

Death was taken aback. "Really?"

"I suppose I should say: on account of you. Mama did an unusual amount of planting and gardening early in the spring. I think—you know, she wanted to see a lot of things growing all around because of Papa. You know, Life in the face of—" he braced himself— "in the face of Death."

"Oh," said Death, and though there was no particular expression in his voice, Xavier felt a little corny.

"I helped her now and then. Not too much, but some. I used to come out here at night and water and weed. Do you know what I did once? Strange that I don't even feel embarrassed telling you this. I jerked off into the earth around the rose bushes. I thought it would make them grow better."

"Maybe it has. They are certainly lovely."

After a while, Xavier asked, "Do many people see you and talk to you?"

"There aren't too many romantics left nowadays. I run into a lot of fortune-tellers, of course, but they're usually after a favor."

"Oh, I'm no romantic," said Xavier. "Not at all. I can't love at all. I mean, if it were possible, I'd marry a dark alley or a waterfront. Not a human being."

Death said, "I'll have to leave you now."

"I won't see you again? I mean, will I ever see you again?"

"I don't know."

"Will you tell me something?"

"If I can."

"Why does it happen? Why is there death?"

"People always ask me that. It's so odd that they think I would know."

"Can't you tell me anything?"

"You're beginning to sound like a fortune-teller. I don't have any answers. Of course I don't have any questions either. I'm in the dark, just like you. I don't make anything happen. Look!" He opened his hand. The rose and the small jewel of blood were unchanged. "Good night, Xavier."

"My real name is Dickie."

Death smiled. "Good night," he repeated.

They were standing beside the mulberry tree. Death walked across the garden and went through the break in the hedge that Xavier had made as a child. He went up the porch steps.

Xavier returned to where he had been sitting before he offered Death the rose, but as he sank into the grass row, the lights went on in the windows overhead and lit the garden up. Shivering, he got back on his feet and started to the front of the house. He changed his mind, suddenly terrified of running into Death. He ran around back and went in through the kitchen.

The nurse was coming out of Papa's room.

"Phone the doctor," she said. "I think it's over."

Xavier glanced at the electric clock on the kitchen wall. It was ten minutes after two. The second hand caught his attention as it ticked downward and he felt himself falling with it.

"Are you going to be sick?" the nurse asked.

He shook his head. "Where is my mother?"

"She's asleep. Phone the doctor first, though."

Xavier crossed the hall from the kitchen and went into his bedroom, followed by the nurse. The lights were off now, except for the bedside lamp. Everything was red. The nurse had covered his father's face, but his feet were sticking out from the bottom of the sheet.

"Cover his feet, for God's sake!" cried Xavier and his brain went dragging with the second hand again.

The nurse tugged at the sheet. "Please phone the doctor."

As Xavier entered the living room, he heard Mama coming down the stairs. She and the nurse reached the living room at the same moment, though from opposite directions. Her hair was wild from sleep and she wore an almost transparent blue nightgown with a blue satin ribbon at the neck. Her flat broad feet were naked. She looked from Xavier to the nurse, from one to the other.

The nurse nodded solemnly. "I think it's over."

Mama clapped her hands together, lifted them to just below her chin, rolled her eyes upward, and said ecstatically, "Thank God."

She was understood to mean: thank God his suffering has ended. But it fell badly from her mouth, and a wave of nausea brought Xavier's supper sourly into his throat. Mama's rehearsals showed. Perhaps she had been preparing her statement for months, perhaps for all her married life. Perhaps she had only prepared it as she came down the stairs. In any case, the Widow had made her Entrance, and spoken her first Speech.

Xavier continued on his way to the telephone.

20

They draped all the mirrors with sheets so that the ghost wouldn't catch a glimpse of himself in passing and thus see his death in his face and suffer the knowledge of it.

Smoking quietly with his hat on, Uncle George sat all night in Xavier's room with the corpse. Not even the little lamp was lit.

Early in the morning, the undertakers came to wash and dress the body. Somehow they banged Papa's head against the wall and the clunk resounded through the house. Uncle George, who had been helping, ran out of the room with his hand in front of his mouth, saying, "If he wasn't dead already, they'd have killed him for sure."

Aunt Faye arrived in time for coffee, and having

drunk, she went to see the corpse. She screamed and wailed hysterically until someone told her to shut up.

The house was full of people. Xavier didn't know half of them, but he hated all of them because they were witnesses to his shame, which was: that his father was dead.

It was a lovely day. People exclaimed in disbelief that on such a day a man should be dead! Friends and strangers gathered in front of the house where the hearse waited. Xavier looked down at them from the window and saw Sissy Applebaum swinging on the garden gate. He was shocked into rage, but did nothing about it. Sissy was laughing and waving to some girl friends across the street. Suddenly, almost everyone seemed jolly.

Alone in the toilet Xavier cried. He didn't know whether he was crying out of humiliation or because Papa was dead. But he cried, flushing and flushing so no one would hear him.

The proceedings were delayed for three hours as his brother-in-law Hank who lived in Newark had to kiss some politician's ass before he could drive his wife into Brooklyn. She was too upset to take the train. And she didn't trust any drivers but her husband, so she couldn't take a taxi.

Finally, they arrived. His sister, who had hated Papa, flew into the house sobbing and shrieking. She and Mama fell together, sobbing and shrieking. All the women began sobbing, and many of them shrieked. Except his sister-in-law Francine who loved the opera. She looked around, trying to catch an eye, so that she could exchange a glance with somebody over the uncouthness of the scene.

The open coffin was brought into the living room by the undertakers and laid across some chairs. It could not be sealed until a member of the family checked the body over. Hank volunteered. He looked. He said, "There are pieces of crockery on his eyelids." Then he turned away, went to a corner of the room, kicked the wall and cried, "How can such a thing happen to a man?" Xavier tried to believe in Hank's performance, especially as he saw Francine being scornful. But he couldn't. He watched coldly and despised him.

The service began. It was brief and in Hebrew. A strange man made a speech which was completely irrelevant. Perhaps he had come to the wrong funeral. He seemed to be talking about a little boy.

Afterwards, everybody went out into the street and the coffin was shoved into the hearse.

Members of the family, with ragged black ribbons pinned to their chests, walked behind the hearse as far as the tiny synagogue a few blocks away. The day was hot and Xavier was embarrassed. He kept his eyes on the asphalt. At the synagogue, the door of the hearse was opened. And the door of the synagogue was opened.

Then everyone climbed into limousines and drove to Long Island for the burial.

On the way back Xavier landed in the same limousine as Hank, two brothers and fat greasy cousin Steve, the family lawyer. Xavier immediately closed his eyes and pretended to be asleep. "What do you think Pop was worth?" Hank asked. Someone made a short embarrassed giggle. But no one answered. Steve whispered to Hank, "See me later." Then Hank began bragging about the big business deal he had concluded that morning.

Xavier fell asleep before he had heard much of it. As he started dozing, he thought, "At last I am free." He fell asleep contented.

21

Carrying Mary and the children piggyback, Tomtom Jim splashed around in the river for a very long time, perhaps hours. The moon had set, which meant that dawn was close.

Mary noticed this and asked, "When do we reach the frontier?"

"We're in the frontier."

"Oh," said Mary, looking back.

Her feet were dragging in the water and she was trembling with cold. "Are you sure you know where you're going?"

Tomtom Jim was so offended by the question that he didn't answer her. The river suddenly deepened and Mary's legs went under up to the knees. Thank God it was too dark to see Baby's face as he chewed on her nipple. She was sure he would have an eyebrow raised mockingly. At her other breast, pretty little Bijou, the apple of her father's eye, lay fast asleep.

22

On the wall opposite the bed was a crucifix whose rugged boyish Jesus was more than three feet high. He was clean shaven, had a crew cut, and wore a white terry-cloth hand towel around his muscular waist. In the gray morning light now filling the attic of St. Francis' Aviary, Jesus looked sad and rather exhausted as if he had just lost a strenuous tennis match. Actually, however, like John Anthony on the narrow cot across from him, he was asleep.

Except for the crucifix, every inch of wall was covered by masks. Hundreds of them, all made by John Anthony at the long worktable near the window. Among the masks were saints, freaks, demons, princesses, movie stars and heroes. But there weren't too many of these. Mostly, the faces were of ordinary people, with a variety of everyday expressions, of which horror, pain, greed and nothing were the most common.

Behind the masks, the walls held a number of hidden speakers. At night, if John Anthony was in the right mood alone or had an especially sensitive visitor, which wasn't often, he would throw a red chiffon cloth over the lampshade and set the small light below Jesus' feet. The room turned pink, the Savior crimson. Then John Anthony would put a requiem or a mass on the tape recorder and connect the machine to the speakers. Instantly the faces burst into song. Their lips moved. The walls lived.

This attic, which was John Anthony's only home, his studio, his refuge and his prison, was also because of limited space the Aviary's Clothing Distribution Center. Or rather, the floor was. Gifts of old clothes came from the rich for the poor, but the poor wouldn't have all of it. They took only what was most respectable. The Birds, even the Lady Birds and the outrageous male ones known as Birds of Paradise, insisted that Bowery wear must be sober and discreet. No fantasy. The cops didn't like it. So month by month, year by year, the attic floor grew higher and more dazzling, like a graveyard of old operas. A pair of blue pantaloons here, a gold brocade kaftan there. Jeweled shoes, feathered boas, elaborate wigs, spectacular hats. Ripped embroideries, bald velvets, tattered damasks, torn lace. The gorgeous dreameries of the rich.

John Anthony awoke, feeling happy and cozy with

his hands clasped between his thighs. "I thank you, dear God, for having made me fail in all things of this world," he said with his head under the blanket.

He let go a chain of farts which he sniffed with pleasure though guiltily, for a woman he'd once been married to had tormented him for enjoying such frightful smells. He couldn't help it. He'd been born a Jew, under the sign of Virgo besides, so he felt very much concerned with what went on inside him.

On account of all the farting, the sniffing, the guilt and the memory of his origins, his morning erection deflated, unloading the collapsed hull in his warm hand. This tempted him to masturbate, which was the only kind of love he'd made since his conversion, but he'd been planning to go to confession that night. It was a week since he went last. He totted up his score, imagining the priest's weary voice coming through the partition: "How many times, my son?"

Sixteen seemed much more terrible a figure than fifteen. And fifteen didn't seem so bad if he actually desisted from sixteen.

In spite of the arithmetic, he was already reaching for the cold cream and the hand mirror when Jesus came to his rescue by stirring, stretching, waking to a new day on the cross. John Anthony heard him, peeked out and smiled like a father. He had spent a whole year carving Jesus from a single perfect oak log, and he'd made a complete man of him. He'd even carved a few drops of sweat between the high tough buttocks and one tiny crab among the pubic hair, invisible unless pointed out.

"Morning, Johnny!" said Jesus, the loosely knotted towel slipping ever so slightly down the narrow hips.

"Morning—" John Anthony clenched his teeth. The name was hot coals in his mouth. Don't say it, don't say it. It fell out. "—Dickie."

Dear God, forgive me! He buried his head under the blanket again and all the happiness and coziness drained out of him. He felt empty. It was the same thing every morning. He shut his eyes tight and muttered something about the Divine Emptiness, the True Nothingness, the Perfect Selflessness. But it didn't do him any good. He felt empty, and this made him feel sad.

"All right, give yourself to your sadness then," he counseled and sank into a vat of sweet and sour sorrow.

He was forty years old and none of his dreams had come true. He was a saint and all he'd ever wanted was to be a sinner. Satan had tricked him, married him and tricked him. The Devil plays dirty! With his long tail up your hungry ass, the contract is consummated. Your black seed splatters the bloody night. You raise your eyes expecting to be luxuriously damned, and behold! you are poor and holy.

John Anthony had meant to be worldly, to live on those portions of the earth that were advertised in magazines, written about in society columns, where men and women as spectacular as their clothes dined on flowered terraces under the stars, died young and dramatically, boated, swam, drove fast cars across continents, were glamorously bored, did degenerate things in candlelit palaces while wearing only pearls or emeralds.

Money, he thought bitterly. It was just money that lifted into its hands the same dull clay of which Adam was made, and shaped it into THEM.

"No, no!" he cried. He couldn't stand the idea that it should be money. He wanted it to be Magic. It was Magic that made them, not money. They were Enchanted, not merely rich, and they lived in an Enchanted Kingdom.

As a youth he had gone through the gates of the Enchanted Kingdom. A few older men and women had kindly offered him their cold hands and led him inside. Rome. Paris. Venice. Gstaad. The Riviera. Those were the places then. But he never enjoyed himself. He was always with the wrong people, and though the right people were within sight, within arm's reach, John Anthony was too shy to move toward them. He sat and lay with the old and the ugly. He might just as well have been in Miami Beach.

And why did the right people never reach for him?

Though he was handsome and elegant and had, he'd often been told, *I am hung like a horse* written in bright red letters across his heavy, sensual face, he was filled with serious weaknesses. He was sweet, but charmless and excessively ingratiating. He had a nervous stomach and couldn't tolerate fancy food or alcohols, or even wine. He was afraid of airplanes, cars, marihuana, boats, everything. He had a terrible memory, practically no powers of observation, no sense of humor, and a kind of vagueness, a gluey wetness in the brain that made his halting conversations uninteresting as well as incomprehensible. He was a drag, and he knew it.

The old and the ugly didn't mind, but he minded them. He believed in love. He wanted to live with someone he loved, someone from among the right people. So he never stayed long with his lovers. A month or two, a short trip, and he'd again be throwing his clothes and books of poetry into a suitcase. Back to a small room in a cheap hotel, his rings and watches pawned. At night he would go to the fashionable bars and shyly wait for the next kind hand. Hoping, hoping, it would be warmer than the last.

He was living with a Bulgarian prince in Paris when he met Dickie Gold, another gigolo but a much more successful one. Much much more successful. Dickie was being kept by three different people at the same time, of whom two were being kept themselves and the third was an Italian movie star. Dickie was gold, and also black. He looked angelic and cruel. He looked innocent and corrupt. A wolf, a tiger, an eagle, a pussycat, a silver goatling. A vampire with honey on its teeth. Dickie was perfect. Smooth, eloquent, strong in the stomach, daring. He sweated charm. Everyone wanted him.

John Anthony wanted him too, terribly, terribly. And one drunk evening they went to bed together in Dickie's house. Hardly anything happened. Dickie was frank. He couldn't get too excited unless somewhere along the line he was getting paid for it. Money made it dirty, and if it wasn't dirty, it wasn't fun. Oh, no, of course he couldn't accept money from John Anthony. That would seem awfully phony. So what could they do? Well, there was one thing Dickie liked . . . He brought a jar of cold cream from the bathroom. Now, this is what you do—

John Anthony slathered up their crotches and, using both hands, jerked the two of them off. Dickie lay there more or less like a corpse, saying no occasionally. No fucking, no sucking, no kissing. No coming at the same time either for that matter because at the last minute Dickie wanted a finger up his ass. Yes, that's it, all the way up. Ah. Ouch, your fingernail! Ooooh. Pass me that towel, will you? Oh, sorry, I didn't realize you hadn't finished. No, go on, I'll get the towel myself. God, all this gook. It seems so foul afterwards. Want a cigarette? What, *still* not done?

It was the most beautiful and romantic night of John Anthony's life. He pestered Dickie for more such nights, and of course Dickie became more and more annoyed and finally refused to see him at all, not even as friends. John Anthony wrote feverish love letters, slipped poems under Dickie's door, phoned him constantly, followed him on the street, haunted the bars and restaurants for a sight of his gold-black darling. On the sidewalk in front of Dickie's house, John Anthony wrote in large chalk letters: "You are the one and only passion of my life, the only thing that has ever happened to me. You are my World War, my Wall Street Crash, my oil well, my career, my family, my religious conversion." Dickie, however, was away at the time, and the rain washed off the statement before he came home.

The Bulgarian prince, exasperated finally, threw John Anthony out. It was winter and very cold; that was practically all he remembered of this period. And that he went every day to a fat blond clairvoyant named Mme. Boeuff for help. None of her magic potions worked, nor her charms, nor her incense fires, nor her Chinese cabinet. Dickie still refused to see him. When John Anthony accused Mme. Boeuff of being a fraud, she tore his cheeks with her fingernails and screamed that he was in the clutches of the Devil, and that only the Devil could make Dickie his.

How? What should he do? He read books on demonology in the Bibliotheque Nationale, knowing full well that everyone else sitting at those long tables under the green shaded lamps was there for the same reason: to find out how to get Dickie. Get Dickie! The alarm struck through mankind's blood. All humanity was John Anthony's rival.

At last, in one book, he found mention of The Black Wedding. Ever after, he wondered why this particular recipe appealed to him. In Bavaria during the seventeenth century, a girl named Anna Weigel who had been spurned by her lover was found in the woods by some farmers. Wearing a black wedding dress, she was walking around in a trance with a black billy goat under her skirts. The goat was killed at once. Anna confessed that she was marrying Satan in order to get her lover back. By order of the Inquisitor, she was fed one thousand needles and then burned at the stake.

John Anthony left the Bibliotheque at once and went

to a secondhand shop where he bought a black satin dress and a thick black veil. Embarrassed, he explained to the proprietor it was for his concierge whose husband had just died. Then he waited until midnight. With the package under his arm, he walked east along the quays until he felt Satan giving him a sign. He went down the steps of the embankment. It was pitch dark and freezing cold. A film of ice was forming on the river.

Under a bridge, he found a small hollow in the embankment. He stepped inside and stripped down to his underwear and shoes. Out of habit, he folded his clothes neatly before piling them on the ground. He pulled on his wedding dress and covered his head with the veil. What now? Where was Satan? Perhaps he was there, further down the embankment where those lights flickered.

John Anthony walked toward the lights, and to his surprise saw that they were fires. There seemed to be figures moving around the flames. Could those be cauldrons steaming? Could that be Hell? He hesitated fearfully, and then he heard a dragging sound behind him. There was a smell of sulphur in the air—and something else. Maybe brimstone. John Anthony, however, wasn't sure he knew what brimstone smelled like.

He longed to turn around, and yet he didn't dare. So he waited. And gradually he realized that something was moving at his feet. He looked down nervously and gasped. Was it a rope, a snake? It was difficult to tell in the dark but—his heart jumped so powerfully that spots danced in front of his eyes. For he had seen the pointed tip. Satan's tail was slithering out from behind him, stretching out across the stones. Suddenly it began to climb. A cold slimy thing twining up his legs, around and around, crawling up his dress. It gave a tug as it encircled his thighs, and he knew what it wanted.

John Anthony hiked up his skirt and bent over. He was as excited as on the night he'd spent with Dickie. His asshole sprang open like a trapdoor. The smell of sulphur and brimstone modulated into the smell of cold cream. Dickie and Satan were one. The tail shoved itself inside John Anthony, continued twisting and climbing. It was surely infinite. It rose inside him, though still winding up his legs. He felt it nudge through his intestines. The night turned red. The tail was in his stomach now, rising toward his throat. The flames ahead flared higher. He was gagging on it.

"God, oh God," John Anthony cried ecstatically.

He came. A crowd of tiny black moths sprang out of him and flew toward the fires. The tail disappeared, within and without.

Exhausted, John Anthony dropped to his knees. His whole body was throbbing now, but he knew he must go on to the fires. He lifted himself unsteadily and began staggering along the embankment.

The fires weren't hell at all. A priest with a beard was tending them. He was boiling soup in cauldrons over them. He was warming a hundred ragged and shivering bums with them. The bums sat on wood and newspapers inside the circle of fire.

John Anthony began to cry silently behind his veil. He couldn't remember the last time he had thought of someone other than himself. He had forgotten other people.

"You forget them every morning," Jesus said.

John Anthony climbed out of bed at last and pulled his clothes on. God, they stank. He'd hunt around on the floor later for something clean.

From the stairway, he smelled coffee percolating and remembered that he'd allowed the Cardinal to spend the night on the sofa in the Recreation Room. He passed this sofa on the way to the toilet and shuddered. In the toilet he peed and washed his face and hands. Before continuing downstairs he stopped into his office to see if the Cardinal had poked around in his papers. (He still wrote love poems to Dickie, though of course he didn't mail them any more. Even after all this time, he knew where Dickie was—managing an art gallery uptown.) The poems seemed untouched.

John Anthony went down to the dining room. The Cardinal was in back, in the kitchen area, hacking up loaves of bread.

Through the door and show windows, John Anthony saw the crowd of Birds waiting to come in for breakfast, their faces pressed against the glass so that they looked like the Cardinal. The Cardinal looked like a little boy with his face pressed against a window.

Staring at his assistant, he thought of Dickie again and a lump came into his throat. It required an effort of will to drag himself across the dining room and into the present. The Cardinal began chatting happily at once. He loved John Anthony. John Anthony took down the eggbeater and started whisking it in the pot of powdered milk and hot water.

23

"What? Tell me! What is he saying?" asked Mary, pulling on Tomtom Jim's sleeve.

"Fuck off!" Tomtom Jim said sharply but without turning his head to her. "You're tipping the boat." He continued talking in a foreign language to the boatman who was rowing them across the enormous lake.

At the other shore, which was drawing closer, Mary could already see the wood. There seemed to be no houses at all, no sign of life. She didn't like the looks of the place, especially since it was heavily covered by clouds. The lake and the land behind her lay under a cloudless blue sky and a warm sun. Mary looked down at the children so as not to have to look ahead. They were asleep—or at least Bijou was. Probably Baby was asleep as well, although his eyes were open.

A wind rose suddenly. The broad brim of the boatman's black hat wriggled and his mustache lifted at the edges. Mary shuddered. She didn't like the man at all. She didn't like the place they were going to.

The conversation between Tomtom Jim and the boatman had apparently ended. Mary leaned forward. "What did he tell you?"

Tomtom Jim turned around and smiled. "He said we shouldn't go into the Black Forest. As if he could scare us!"

"What does he row people there for if he doesn't think they should go in?" she asked.

Tomtom Jim spoke to the man briefly and then told Mary: "He says he has to earn his living."

"I see," she said coldly. It was always the same story. A crow had given them the address of a fortune-teller for a bag of corn, but warned them not to see her. The fortune-teller wanted a dollar before telling them where to find a certain waiter, but warned them not to see him. The waiter, for another dollar, directed them to a cathedral where, by throwing some money into a poorbox, a statue of St. Stanislaus told them where to go, but also warned them against going.

"Fairyland," the statue had said, "is where you can look down on the stars. But you better not go there."

Mary could no longer remember all the stages of their pilgrimage, and in truth she was getting tired of the whole thing. Besides, she suspected she was pregnant again.

They were still quite a distance from land when the boatman drew in his oars and sprang out of the boat. The water came up only to his thighs. He pulled the boat in with one hand, and then politely helped his passengers ashore. Bijou, who had awakened, went first. Though she couldn't yet speak, she could walk, and so was well inland by the time the others disembarked.

"Is the boatman going to wait for us?" Mary asked.

"He says he only rows people over, not back."

"And what are *we* supposed to do?" she snapped.

"Don't use that tone of voice with me or I'll kick you in the ass. Remember, this whole thing is your idea. We're supposed to look for a man in a wall."

"But there isn't a house in sight."

"That's what I said, but he said we'd find him all right, and it was better if we didn't."

Meanwhile, the boatman had pushed his boat out again and was now climbing into it. They watched him go. Even Bijou stopped and looked. Even Baby, with a little smile, turned from Mary's nipple and watched the boat and the boatman grow smaller and brighter. Around the family all was silence except for the sighing of the wind and the soft drumming of thunder.

Just above the shore, where the land became less marshy, was a footpath, and this they followed, for it seemed to lead straight to the Black Forest. On the plains around them the grass and shrubbery were black.

Mary walked with her shoulder touching Tomtom Jim's arm and she kept calling Bijou to stay close to them.

"What a funny place this is," said Tomtom Jim in a whisper.

Steeling themselves, the pilgrims continued along the path, and soon they were at the mouth of the forest where the pitch-black tamaracks seemed topless. They stepped forward, but didn't have the impression of entering. Rather, they felt as if they were being swallowed by the wood, sucked into it.

It was an unusual place in many ways other than the color and height of the trees. The earth, if you could call it that, was a solid slab of translucent blue stone, and except for the the tamaracks, whose roots were visible under the forest floor, there was no vegetation at all. Not a bush nor a fallen leaf. Not even any little trees. The light in the wood was yellow, and it didn't come in from above, nor from anywhere else apparently. It was just there, gentle and asleep, like a cat. But the most curious thing of all was that there was no smell of any kind. Mary and Tomtom Jim both noticed this at the same time. Together they sniffed. Then Mary leaned over and sniffed at his armpit.

"Nothing," she said. "Not a thing."

Tomtom Jim then knelt down and stuck his head up Mary's skirt.

"Hardly anything," he said, getting up.

But Mary could tell he was just being polite. Feeling terrible, she pretended to be interested in the height of the trees.

Suddenly the yellow air darkened and turned green. It began to rain—sideways.

"Look!" cried Tomtom Jim. "There's a cave over there!"

He grabbed Mary's hand and she grabbed Bijou's, and since she now had both arms extended Baby had no further support. He hung on to her nipple, biting it hard. Mary screamed and Baby fell, practically tearing her tit off as he went. She picked him up at once. He didn't cry but he spat in her face.

"He seems all right," said Mary.

The little family hurried through the trees toward the rise of blue stone which Tomtom Jim had pointed to. It was open on one side like a hood.

"I'm drenched to the skin," Mary complained as they entered. "And so are the children."

"We better all take our clothes off and let them dry," said Tomtom Jim.

The cave was much larger than had appeared from outside, and it was full of yellow light. When the four of them were naked, Tomtom Jim spread their clothing out on the floor, took the knife from his pants pocket and said, "I'll go have a look around and see how deep this thing goes."

Mary stood there shivering and waiting and wishing she were back in New York. To pass the time she began thinking about the avenues and streets of her native city. Oh, how I would love a hot dog at Nathan's or a hamburger at Grant's or a big plate of potato salad at the New York Delicatessen or a dry martini anywhere.

"Hey, Mary!" Tomtom Jim's voice woke her from her reverie. "Come and see what I found."

Gathering her children, Mary walked fearfully into the depths of the cave. Soon the yellow light grew brighter and more luminous, almost like sunlight. Tomtom Jim was standing alongside a big hole in the ground, and when Mary approached and looked into it, she found a broad blue stone stairway that went straight down. It seemed like an interminable stairway and made her dizzy just to look at it.

"I bet that's the road to fairyland," said Tomtom Jim.

"Fairyland?" Mary repeated vaguely.

"Shall we?" Tomtom Jim said gaily and offered her his arm.

"Oh, of course!"

And they started down the stairs.

Fairyland, fairyland, Mary thought. Was that what they were looking for? It took a certain effort to remember the reason for their travels. Her baby! Her little boy! Could it be, was he there waiting for her somewhere at the bottom of those steps?

Down the blue stone stairs they went, naked, growing hungry and tired as hours turned into days and days into weeks.

24

Reason told them that if there were steps, the steps must lead somewhere, and so they persevered. But each day made them more skeptical.

Often they stopped and slept on the cold translucent stone. More often they despaired.

"Maybe we should turn back," said Mary. But when she looked up and saw how high they must climb to go back to the beginning, she shook her head hopelessly.

Thirsty, hungry, exhausted, the little family persevered.

And one day, finally, at long last, they saw far below them a pool of red light. It was perhaps another week before they reached it: a large bare chamber of red stone and red light. It was like being inside a ruby.

"Nothing," Mary whimpered. "Just more nothing. Only red."

At that moment, Bijou let out a wail of fright.

One of the red walls was an enormous living face with red eyes that moved and a mouth that opened on a huge red tongue and big red teeth.

Tomtom Jim flicked his knife open.

25

The sky was already beginning to darken, and John Doe still hadn't said a word. He hadn't said a word since he'd walked in. He sat at the bridge table filling the room up with cigar smoke and finishing one glass of milk and whiskey after the other. The silence made James Madison feel naked. A few minutes ago he had felt so naked that he'd almost jumped off the cot and run into the other room. But his very nakedness paralyzed him. He wished he had some new underwear, but he'd given up the hope of ever getting any.

Since the room was growing darker, he now found the courage to speak. "What's the matter with you today anyway?"

"Nothing," he said. He sounded a little too casual.

"Are you tired, or what?"

"Yes, perhaps a little tired."

"You don't feel like doing anything today?"

"I'm doing everything I want to do right now. I always do exactly what I want to do."

"Oh," said James Madison. "I guess you had a hard day at the office, or wherever you work. You do have a job, don't you?"

"You know that's none of your business."

Why did he sound so funny and cool? "It's getting hotter and hotter these days. I bet its August already. The sun comes in in the morning for a little while, and it gets real hot but I lie in it. Do you think I'm tanned at all? It's too dark to tell now, but maybe you noticed before."

"To tell the truth, I didn't."

Maybe he doesn't like me any more? James Madison asked himself, stumbling over the word "like." It seemed embarrassingly personal, and he tried to re-phrase the question, but even as he sought a more appropriate word, panic began rising up inside him. He said, "Is that what it is? You had a bad day?"

"No, not at all."

"Maybe you had a hard night?"

"Yes, that's it." He seemed a little better now, more like himself. "I had a very hard night. My boyhood chum and his wife came to dinner. He's a major general now, attached to the Pentagon. What are you looking so blank for? Don't you know what the Pentagon is? Do you know who the President of the United States is? Have you ever heard of the United States?"

"I'm not very interested in mathematics or politics."

"What does interest you? Does anything in this wide world interest you?"

Again that cool creepy tone! James Madison felt like bursting into tears. He wanted to fly across the room and hurl himself at John Doe's feet and say, You interest me. Nothing in the world interests me except you. He believed, however, that to do this was against all the laws of the universe. So he said, "I like to sleep because this mattress is lumpy and makes me dream. I'm also beginning to like those pills a lot. They make me dream too."

"But after all—the world outside! Aren't you curious about that?"

"What world outside? Have I ever been out of this room?"

"That's a strange question. Do you imagine you were born here?"

Things were slipping inside James Madison. "Wasn't I?" he wailed.

"How would I know? But in any case, you are interested in your dreams. So tell me, what are they about?"

Drawers opened, cards shuffled, locks snapped, and a strange wind swept through his body, bringing with it a wave of such agony that he sat up and doubled over. "I never dream," he cried out. "It's a lie. I don't have any desires or any hopes. I want nothing. I love no one. I'm only pretending to be a human being. I'm not one and never have been one. I think maybe I'm a spy from another planet or another kind of life, but if I am, then I've forgotten what or who I'm spying for. All I know is that I'm no one, no one at all, nameless and faceless."

John Doe was taken aback. "Maybe you ought to see a psychiatrist," he said gently. "Do you know what that is?"

The tenderness in his voice caused James Madison to sit up and stretch his arms out. "Would you like me to to different?" he asked humbly.

John Doe heaved a sigh of relief, then slammed his hand down on the bridge table. The bottles and glasses clanked against each other. "I don't give a shit who or what you are. As far as I'm concerned—"

"Tell me about your friend the major general," said James Madison, lying down again.

"What friend?"

"The one who came to supper last night and that's why you're so tired."

The room was almost altogether in darkness now. "Oh, yes, Dickie . . . he has red hair and very white skin and freckles. He still looks the way he did when he was fifteen years old, except sexier because he's more of a man. He wears his uniform tight and always sits with his legs apart so you can see how he's hung."

"Big, huh?" James Madison's genitals shriveled up. "As big as you?"

"Bigger, even bigger."

"Impossible!"

"How would you know, you ass?"

James Madison pulled the dark over himself and was silent.

"Oh, that uniform gets me hot. When a uniform fits right—mmm! Around those great shoulders and strong thighs. That's what I really want to find, someone who's even more of a man than I am. We had strawberry shortcake for dessert. Then we left the ladies in the dining room and went into my study for drinks. Or we pretended it was for drinks.

"We sat down on the floor the way we used to when we were kids. And we called each other Huck and Tom the way we used to, although his name is Dickie and my name of course isn't Tom. I brought out my collection of pornographic pictures and showed him the ones I knew he'd like best, the ones with women in them. Cunt. Lots of gaping wide-eyed cunt. Does the idea of it make you sick?"

"Who, me?"

"Yes, *you.*"

"Yes, it sounds disgusting. Horrible."

"Well, he's a man, and men like it. He sat there moaning and rubbing himself. I know how to stir him up. I can be something of a coquette myself, you know. I can make myself wanted. And he was wanting. Before we'd even come to the last of the photographs, he was looking me hard in the eyes and panting.

" 'Let's go!' he yelled and we leaped at each other and tore each other's clothes off. We did everything, everything you can possibly imagine—real things, real sex, real meat. *He did me.* Again and again, with my legs up on his shoulders and my beautiful black hair spreading on the carpet and a pillow under my hips. Thunder and lightning! He ripped me open and in tearing ecstasy I screamed, Huck fuck suck buck schmuck muck tuck cluck wuck etcetera. Because the loves of our youth are the ones we never recover from. They're the only ones that ever matter. All the rest are games and shadows."

Even in the dark John Doe could see the tears sparkling in James Madison's eyes.

"Does that story make you feel bad?" he asked. "Does it make you feel human?"

26

Dickie Gold. Where was he? What had become of him?

The memory seized Baby harshly, sprang out at him from nowhere, brought him to a standstill on the crowded street. After the initial shock, he felt beautiful, a slim graceful boy with powerful hands, a young emperor on a caparisoned horse. He gave off a smell of spiced soaps and perfumed creams. But standing there bloated and bulging on the walk, he was in everyone's way. People complained, poked him with their elbows. Baby edged over into a storefront.

Unexpectedly, he caught sight of himself in the show window and had to look away. No, no, he couldn't be that overblown balloon from some old Macy's Thanksgiving Day Parade. He waited, then drew up close to the window so that he was looking into the reflection of his eyes framed by their butterfly glasses. In his eyes, he saw his own suffering and pleading beauty. "Be me, be me," his beauty implored him, crying out of the pale lusterless pupils.

He must find Dickie. But where? It was years since he'd seen him. Baby couldn't remember how much time had passed nor under what circumstances they had separated. Had there been violence? A drunken brawl perhaps which ended with Dickie stabbing him? Or him stabbing Dickie? Maybe not. Baby seemed to recall that Dickie had gone on to a career in Hollywood and had gradually faded out of his life. Yes, that was it—or was it?

Baby remembered an in-person appearance at the Paramount with enormous posters and teen-age girls lining up all the way down Forty-third Street and around Eighth Avenue. The girls laughed and laughed at the big fat man who waited patiently in line with them. Little did they know, Baby thought now as he had then, tears welling up in his eyes.

Dickie came out on the stage and the girls howled like wolves, stamped their feet, rolled in their seats and in the aisles. A smell of fish and perfume spread through the Paramount. An evil smell. It smelled like Pandora's box. And there was Dickie the good, the pure, the royal, the holy, waving his arms in a golden spotlight. He wore a striped seersucker jacket and white ducks, an old-fashioned straw hat. In one hand he carried a cane, and in the other a small bouquet of forget-me-nots. Had he spotted Baby? Baby didn't know for sure, but when Dickie sang "I'll never smile again" his eyes were fixed on the fifth row center where Baby sat sobbing his heart out amidst the hysterical girls.

He hadn't gone backstage after the show. The past was the past, after all.

Or no—Dickie hadn't turned into a movie star, had he? Maybe he'd gone into some kind of business, electrical supplies, something like that.

The more Baby thought about it, the more confused he became. He must find Dickie. He *would* find him too, even if he had to search in every corner of the world. At least it would give him something to do. Stepping from the storefront with new purpose and fresh energy, Baby bounded and bumped through the crowds, up the street to a telephone booth. Inside, he tore pages out of the directory.

By eleven o'clock that night, he had visited the homes of twenty persons named Richard Gold. Some of the Richards were children, some were dead. One had moved. A number of them were at work and he had to come a second time to take a look. Baby was somewhat devious in his methods until the doors opened. Then he was direct. He explained that he was looking for an old buddy whom he hadn't seen in years. A certain Richard Gold. Sorry to stop by in these clothes, but I drive a cab and I just had a fare in this neighborhood. A man and a woman. I heard them mention Dickie's name when I drove past this house. I wondered if it could be the same Dickie. No? No, I guess not. Thanks just the same. Sorry to have bothered you.

They all seemed rich and many of them lived in private homes in Brooklyn and the Bronx. He got a few suspicious looks during the day, but not more than he usually did, and one elderly woman even invited him inside to wait and have a cup of coffee. Richard was her brother and would soon be home from the shop. She brought a picture of him in with the coffee. A gaunt embittered face with a hook nose. "Oh no," said Baby. "That's not my Dickie."

Night began to fall. He disturbed people at their suppers and their television sets. The nineteenth and twentieth Richards were in bed when Baby came. They were annoyed. So Baby decided to make only one more call that night. Besides, the twenty-first Richard lived just the other side of Prospect Park from the twentieth, and also twenty-one was his lucky number.

Baby went into the hall of the white brick apartment house, but the lobby door was locked. He had already handled this situation. The house directory on the wall stated that Gold lived in 3C. Baby rang apartment number 8D.

It took a long time before a woman's voice came out of the wall. "Yes? Who's down there?"

"Western Union," Baby said into the speaker.

A buzzer sounded and the door clicked open. Baby walked among the potted plants and took the elevator up to the third floor. He rang apartment C.

Seeing the spy-hole darken, Baby moved aside as he had all day. And then, from the other side of the door, he heard a familiar voice. "Who's there?" the screechy voice asked.

Baby stuttered, "D-D-Dickie?"

The door opened, and for the twenty-first time Baby was disappointed. This Richard Gold was a short fat man with a wide flat face as expressionless as a robber with a lady's stocking over his head. He was wearing an undershirt and his armpits stank. Almost immediately the man's blank face twisted into a look of horror, his mouth opened and he yelled, "Help! "

"Dickie? Is that you?" Baby whispered in astonishment, but not to the man, to someone he thought might be inside the man. "Are you trapped in there? Are you a prisoner?"

The man began pushing the door shut but Baby put his foot against it, and his weight, and the door shot all the way back. Behind the man was a long pale-green corridor.

"Help! Police!" the little man shrieked.

Baby was aware of doors opening around him in the hallway and of neighbors peering out.

"Help! Help!"

Neither the man nor Baby moved.

At the end of the green corridor, a woman appeared, a large fat woman in a pink nightgown with two babies in her arms. She too began screaming. Husband and wife were yielding up nightmare screams. Yet, despite all their terror and desperation, Baby heard in their voices and read in their faces something that said At Last. At Last the faceless nameless horror that lurked, that marched, that ran, that followed, that flowed, that crept under doors, that gnawed, that knocked, that rapped, that sighed, that whispered, that threw its black shadow, that poured its hot breath, that watched from nowhere and everywhere—At Last it had appeared. At Last its presence was upon them.

Me?

Baby Poorpoor thought: Can it be me?

27

Baby hurried through the dark parking lot and crossed
the street, hoping no one would notice him as he entered
the lobby of the Hotel Zanzibar. He kept his eyes on the
stone floor, turned left after five or six yards, raised his
eyes in the dim narrow corridor, and with a sigh of relief
dropped a dime into the coin lock. The men's room
seemed empty. He went into the booth on the left,
dropped his pants out of habit, not because he needed
to, and sat down, panting heavily.

He was already beginning to feel safe. It was warm
and steamy in here, and he liked the smell.

There was a glory hole the size of a quarter in the
partition between the two booths. Ants were coming
out of it. They stood on the ledge of the hole and waved

their antennae before entering. There were quite a number of ants on the walls all around Baby. He watched them and grew calmer and more contented.

Presently, he removed his glasses and put his face close to the hole. On the other side a brown eye looked back at him. The eye withdrew and soon Baby saw a mulatto or a Puerto Rican standing completely naked in the next booth. The mulatto began writhing and moving his hands in a slow, heavy, elegant way, as if he were doing a fan dance. Baby knew what was supposed to happen next. He was supposed to do something inventive for the mulatto to look at. After which they would stick their genitals under the partition.

Suddenly filled with loathing, Baby tore off a piece of toilet paper, chewed it into a wad and plunged it in the glory hole.

The ants went into a frenzy. From all corners of the booth, they began racing toward the hole. They walked on the wet toilet paper plug, smelled it, bit it, waved to each other about it. They couldn't get through it. They couldn't go home. Baby lifted his hand and using the ball of his index finger smashed a dozen ants, one by one.

"Home," he muttered with a shudder at each annihilation. "Now you are home."

Relaxing, he sat back and peed in thin little spurts. It was years since he had peed like any ordinary man. Sometimes he thought he never had. So ashamed was he of his tight miserable spurts that he always avoided urinating in public. I should see a doctor, he told himself as he did every time he peed. And then with a shrug: Oh, it'll last until the mess is over.

He noticed a drop of blood then, one large splash of blood on the tile near the door of the booth. It was almost fresh. He shivered fearfully and began examining himself. No, it wasn't his. Something had happened here in this booth, some violence or sickness, perhaps seconds before he entered. Had the fan dancer witnessed it? Had he perpetrated it?

Baby pulled up his pants and quickly left the booth. Drops of blood led across the toilet floor and outside the toilet, in the lobby, and even out on the street. He followed the dark stains across the concrete, and then the asphalt. Sick with fear, he followed them across the parking lot.

28

Sheets of gray rain were falling through the green trees. The rain fell through the rain.

As the train came out of the tunnel on to the elevated tracks the sunset was bleeding across the city, and the darkening panorama of downtown Brooklyn looked like a rusty junkyard.

The El station swayed in the wind, wrapped in thick fog. The planks creaked and groaned. A girl in a hooded raincoat and high heels tapped her toe anxiously to show she was waiting for someone.

Trapped in the treetops, the fog dripped from the branches onto the streets of the past. In the dark and the mist, the stooped, bent man seemed old. They stopped and looked at each other under the dripping branches.

"I was going for cigarettes," the man said. "I broke up with my wife, and I've come home."

Baby said nothing. They began walking together toward the avenue.

"I see the children on weekends. Only on Sundays to tell the truth. And every Sunday they seem more distant and it takes more hours to get close to them. Of course I have my work and I make a lot of money now. But it's not much of a life. My mother is getting old and she never was much company. It's funny living with her again. But what about you?"

"Me? Oh, me . . ." It was a mistake. He stopped walking and edged sideways to the curb. He felt his legs prepare to run. He didn't know this man. They'd never met before.

"What's the matter?" the man asked.

Baby turned upon him angrily. "Do you know me?"

"Of course I do."

"Who am I?"

The man looked helpless and bent. He looked submissive, destroyed. He looked as if he were asking for pity. "I don't know. I don't remember. I've seen you around. I—does it matter?" he whimpered finally. "What difference does it make?"

They continued walking until they reached the candy store on the corner near the El station.

"How about some ice cream?" the man asked.

They sat down opposite each other in one of the two old booths. The man smelled sweet, perhaps of hair oil or soap, and Baby's heart pounded joyously. On the tabletop their hands met. And then their eyes met. They were silent.

29

Here was the everlasting tree-lined street with its sooth-ing shadows, its tremendous yellow moon, its smell of cut grass and of drenched lilac. Here, age, change and death were gay masks worn by the eternal past so as not to bare its grotesque constancy.

Baby sat in the kitchen eating what was set before him on the white enamel table. There were chopped chicken livers, then chicken soup, then roasted chicken with roasted potatoes, all brought to him on heavy wil-low pattern plates. Mama cleared the table and washed the dishes. She turned on the radio and listened to the news.

He was an interloper, a chance passenger out of a time machine, a persecutor of the eternal past. Somewhere around the house or out in the garden a child he imagined was himself sat trembling behind a snowball tree, trembling with the superstitious fear that through the evil vanity of time he might be forced to impersonate the visiting creature, the hideous impostor out of the machine.

The world's news was bad, little redheads, said the radio in a rich grateful voice. Today there are three new wars, eight revolutions, a hundred uprisings, a thousand floods, fires, plagues, a million mortal accidents.

Mama sat smoking her cigarette cozily. "Nothing changes," she said.

"One day Papa was going to the village with the wagon and the horse to sell cabbages. I was only a little girl, maybe three years old, maybe eight. I begged Papa to take me with him. He didn't want to because it could be dangerous. But anyway he took me. There was a small path from the farm to the road and it had plants with big leaves all along the edges. It smelled so good and fresh. We rode on the wagon down the path, and the sun was shining. I was always happy to be with Papa because I loved him. I didn't love anyone but him. I sang because of the sun and smell and going to the village with Papa. Then we turned off onto the main road. Here it could be dangerous. It went through the middle of a forest. All the land belonged to one man—a prince who lived in Moscow. So we were riding along and all of a sudden a bunch of drunk Russians on horses came galloping out of the trees. I don't remember what happened but I woke up later with blood coming out of my head. You can still see the scar through my hair."

The thought of her childhood nearly broke his heart. A little girl who loved her father. A horse and wagon. The same old sun. Drunk joyous peasants who would soon ride a revolution into the new world.

"Where are you going?" she asked.

"Upstairs. To see Papa."

"Papa is dead."

He climbed the steps and went into the hot rosy room where Papa was eternally dying.

"Hello, Papa."

"Hello, my boy."

"How are you feeling?"

"All right. And you?"

"Not so bad. Not so bad."

"Sit down here a little on the bed."

Baby sat down. Papa too had a childhood—on the Black Sea. He was playing marbles even now in Odessa and Bessarabia, Moldavia and Transylvania. He was planning to go to America, to get rich, to marry, and to die his everlasting death. All the little children were huddling together: the little girl with her head whacked open, the boy on the Black Sea, and the boy trembling somewhere around the house or in the garden.

At midnight Baby left Papa to his death and went downstairs. Mama didn't recognize him. She turned pale to see a stranger in the house.

"It's just me, Mama, your son," he said. "I have to be going now."

"Goodbye, *tottele*," she said, giving him a quarter. "Wrap up well and take care of yourself. The years are getting colder."

30

Madame Madison, in a coat of ermine but naked underneath except for a triple strand of pearls swinging between her breasts, parked her convertible alongside the river in the densest dark of a damp hot night. The night smelled of cucumber, watermelon rind, dill, herring. Rats scampered under the piers. Slither and clump. Unrolled condoms—are any cocks that long? she asked herself—flashed in schools on the surface of the water.

Madame sat hopefully with a volcano rumbling between her thighs. She lit a cigarette, tossed her head, acted elegant.

At last, in the menacing shadows under the overhead highway, a sailor appeared. He was groping himself. Madame Madison stared at him between half-closed lids. The sailor began unbuttoning his fly. Madame stared more insistently, nudging him with her gaze. Go on, go on already, said her eyes.

Knees bent, pelvis arched forward, the sailor with infinite slowness began liberating the thickest, most interminable length of—Was it? Could it be? He exuded it, unwound it. It came like an infinite intestine, like a garden hose. It was dragging on the ground. It would surely take a derrick to lift it. If his penis was any measure, his testicles would be the size of whales.

Gently he stroked himself. And with each interminable stroke, Madame's innards swooned.

"God," she moaned, choking on her own sulphurous fumes. "Good God in heaven."

The sailor sauntered out of the shadows. Stroke swoon. Stroke. Swoon.

"Oh baby baby," he whispered hoarsely. "Here comes Jack the Ripper, Jack the Grim Reaper, Jack the Slim Raper, Jack the Black Wrapper."

She heard Black Wrapper, but he might have meant Black Rapper. In fact that seemed more logical. For a moment Madame was lost in thought. By the time she left her mind, she was enduring but concealing a wave of disgust, for she loathed wise guys and intellectuals. The volcano subsided, smoked petulantly.

Stroke. Nothing. Stroke. *Sssss*. An exciting hiss issued from between the sailor's clenched teeth. Stroke. *Sssss*. Swoon.

He was alongside the convertible now, the infinite phallus still unloading on the ground. Madame flung her cigarette away, casually let her furs fall open. She played with her pearls distractedly, but then, no longer able to conceal her desire, fanned her fingers out under her breasts and lifted them to the night.

"Yes," she cried. "It is enormous. But doesn't it ever get hard?"

Enraged, the sailor turned around and went back to where he had come from, under the elevated highway. He poured himself a milk and whiskey from the bridge table.

Lifting one naked foot, Madame extended her leg along the seat and pushed down the handle with her toes. The door swung open. She stretched herself out on the seat, bent her knees and spread them. She wriggled and squirmed, twisted, ground and gnashed her teeth, shrieked desire so loudly that the rats and condoms fled in panic.

Contempt pulling down the ends of his mouth, the sailor walked over to Madame Madison, stumbling on his genitalia. He slapped her face, tore the pearls from her neck and stuffed them in his back pocket, then pinched and twisted her nipples until her lovely little breasts looked cross-eyed. When at last he stopped tormenting her, she was whimpering, but happily, because she had come.

31

Ferguson turned on the motor, and they sat waiting for it to warm up and for the blades to wipe the windshield clean. The rain sounded like bullets on the roof. Shivering, Andy pressed hard against his father.

"Ooooh, it's so cold," he said.

"Cold, ha! Don't make excuses. You're just a goddamn freak, that's all." He put his arm around the boy's shoulder, pulling him tight. "But so am I."

Andy laughed, his body jerking with giggles and chill. Ferguson hugged him tighter, drowning in love. These moments between the house and Andy's school were always the happiest of Ferguson's day, and yet, once over he never remembered them until he and his son were back in the car. These moments were a thrilling wild beast that could not live in captivity, that could thrive only in its natural habitat.

"My innocent, my darling innocent boy," Ferguson exclaimed, his voice breaking. This was eternal, immutable heaven, sitting with the boy in the car beaten by rain while the motor idled.

"Me—innocent? You think I'm on trial or something?"

"I didn't mean innocent that way," said Ferguson coldly and withdrew his arm. "Innocent is when you believe heaven is where you will be reunited with your loved ones forever, rather than free of them at last."

Instead of going straight to work after dropping Andy, Ferguson drove down to Madison Street. He sat in the gray light and repeated: "I despise you. I loathe you. I despise you . . ."

James Madison slept.

32

Soon it would be dawn, and he didn't have a quarter for the Comet. That meant the Aviary again. Damn, thought Tommy and hugged his knees, feeling like a little boy who had five more long and marvelous minutes before getting out of bed to go to school.

He was sitting under a tree in Union Square and the night, or the morning, was becoming colder. And darker. And damper. On the lawn across the path from him a bunch of bums were lighting a fire in a waste-paper basket. The flames rose with a roar, and Tommy recognized the five wild-eyed people, including the Negro and the woman in the brown cloche hat. He even recognized the brown cloche hat which John Anthony had once tried on for him. For the briefest moment,

Tommy considered going over to the fire and getting happy with the others. He watched enviously as they passed around a bottle of muscatel.

But he didn't move from where he sat. He would feel like an impostor among the bums, unable to share their stupid conversations, their laughter, their rage or self-pity. He would only be able to share their fire and their wine, and they would know this and hate him for it and insult his face.

He had three cents in his coat pocket and another penny hidden in the band of his hat for good luck. If he went and stood outside the subway entrance under the park he could raise the quarter in no time and so be able to spend the day sleeping at the Comet. But he hated begging. He hated sticking his face into people's lives for a nickel or a dime. Anyway, the Aviary wasn't so terrible, if only John Anthony weren't such a pill. Well, there was a price to be paid for everything, even for misfortune. And he knew he ought to be grateful that John Anthony realized he was someone special and treated him accordingly. What other bum was allowed to sleep in the attic and on John Anthony's own bed?

Oh God, the attic, Tommy groaned, and suddenly he was talking to Ismael about it. My dear, that attic! Ragsville, dragsville, schmattaland! It would be marvelous to get stoned on mescaline and spend the night there. Remember, like those nights we used to read Dr. Franzblau to each other, vomiting with laughter. Well, the attic . . . well, it's like a slaughterhouse where a thousand dead queens were beheaded. And their heads are nailed on the walls. Also there's a lewd Christ that looks like it's made of marzipan. Sometimes he wears a towel, sometimes a jock strap, and sometimes absolutely nothing at all.

Poor John Anthony, Tommy thought with a pang of remorse. He was lonely too, despite the mobs at the Aviary, despite his selfless devotion to homeless drunks, despite his Cardinal, his God, his masks, his music. What does it take to fill up a man's life, Tommy wondered, and tried not to remember the answer. But John Anthony is really so silly and vulgar, honestly! Imagine this: he comes slinking into the attic while I'm lying there, licks his lips, slaps his rump and says, "It's not the pain but the strain." Or else he does a clumsy shimmy: "It's not the find but the grind."

The sky had turned gray. Tommy stood up quickly and, after hesitating, gathered up the soggy newspapers he'd been sitting on half the night. He climbed the railing and walked over to the bums. It was delicious near the fire, and he suddenly realized how cold he'd been. He shuddered with pleasure, but also with chill.

The bums were quarreling about China, and Tommy despised them for it. What wouldn't I despise them for? he asked himself, and to his surprise realized that there was something. One thing only: silence.

But now they were shouting at the tops of their voices.

"Here," said Tommy and flung the newspapers into the flames.

As the fire sank, all the five bums looked at him.

"Hello, pretty," the woman in the brown cloche hat said, and smiled.

Tommy turned away.

Leaving the park, he went east along Fourteenth Street and then south on Third Avenue so he could pass the Comet. He paused on the walk in front. The doors and the cashier's box were still closed, but the smell slipped out to greet him. Maybe it really was the worst smell in the world, as he'd once believed—the lowest, the foulest, the most appropriate to his destiny. But Tommy had come to love it. He closed his eyes and breathed deeply, identifying the ingredients like old friends. It was blended as carefully as a Chanel, a Guerlain. The most obvious ingredient was the toilet. It wasn't subtle but it was strong, virile. The weaker scents flew in like violins: armpits, stale cigarette smoke, cruddy balls, drying piss. And then like brass: rotgut whiskey and the poisoned breath of rotting stomachs. And then, like a clash of cymbals: cheesy foreskins.

And strangely, sweetly, underneath the smell was a tissue of real, though cheap, perfume. A floor. A carpet. Yes, Tommy decided, a magic carpet bearing a pack of howling djinns.

He continued on his way downtown, his pace increasing, for the sun was already up and his face was beginning to feel big as it always did during the day.

When Tommy came through the Aviary door, John Anthony dropped his pots and pans and raced across the dining room, clapping his hands together and breaking into smiles. All the Birds eating breakfast turned to look, as did the Cardinal who was serving them. Tommy's face felt enormous.

John Anthony had become very fond of Tommy, and although he knew nothing of his past, he could tell he had been Someone. He had done Something. He came from Somewhere. John Anthony provided Tommy not only with a past but with a history. In the ruined face he saw the crumbling turrets of a castle on a wild northern cliff. Wild, but not too wild. Unkempt was more like it, and barren, with dead trees and dried weeds and bloomless ivy swinging off the walls. In the twists and turns of Tommy's face, John Anthony saw the rise and fall of an ancient house. Twist by twist, turn by turn, it grew mighty, then wore itself out down the ages, emerging proudly and finally in this ultimate degeneracy. Tommy wore his line's corruption like a coat of arms. He was history's paschal lamb, time's sacrifice.

John Anthony longed to make him happy. He knew Tommy's soul was shut and suffering. He longed to open it.

He led Tommy up the two flights of stairs to the attic, chucking him under the chin, winking at him, chattering the latest Aviary gossip. Tommy acted interested and genteel, hating himself. Instead of flinging himself down on the bed the way he wanted to do, he walked around the room and admired the new masks. He could always tell a new one. His intuition had always been extraordinary. In fact, and in the past this used to worry him, he had no taste at all, only intuition.

Sort of casually he worked his way around the room to the cot. Still talking about the masks, he sat down on the coarse brown blanket. Ooooh, that felt good. He leaned over on his elbow. He brought his feet up on the bed, torn shoes and all. Then, inch by genteel inch, he stretched himself out. He rolled over on his back. His hat came down on his face bringing night. Ahhhhh . . .

The conversation took its usual course. John Anthony said, "Come on, take your things off before you fall asleep, you big baby."

Tommy talked through his hat: "I'm used to sleeping in my clothes. You know that. I'd feel funny without them."

"I bet you wouldn't look so funny." He waited. "And you'd be a lot more comfortable. You need a change of clothes anyway. Just look at those shoes! There's nothing left of them. And no socks!"

"I'll change later," Tommy said, and not only because he was shy of undressing in front of John Anthony, but because he hoped later to put on several layers of clothing which he could sell bit by bit at the thieves' market outside the Salvation Army.

"Goodness, and the crotch of your pants is practically gone. I can see your ding-dong."

Tommy brought his legs together and closed his coat. "I promise I'll change later on."

John Anthony clicked his tongue and Tommy knew

he was also shaking his head and pursing his lips. Inside the lovely dark of his hat, he fell asleep.

He was soon awakened by a handsome beefy blond boy in black clothes carrying a bowl of coffee and a chunk of brown bread smeared with margarine. Tommy awoke with an erection and the sight of the boy made him feel he would explode. When the boy leaned forward to hand Tommy the food, a silver crucifix on a chain fell out of his shirt. Tommy also caught a glimpse of his white hairless chest. The boy sat down on the edge of the bed rather heavily, but not gracelessly. He blushed and smiled.

While he ate, Tommy wondered what would happen if he groped the boy, or grabbed him, or even simply flirted a little. He probably knew the score. Everyone did nowadays despite the bullshit at Time, Inc. Besides, John Anthony had told him that all the boys who helped out at the Aviary could be had. But of course John Anthony was another story. He wasn't young any more, but at least he looked human.

Tommy's face swelled suddenly to the size of the room. He wondered what had become of his hat and then saw that it had rolled off the bed. He handed the empty bowl back to the boy, and turned over on his belly. The pillow smelled of cold cream. Tommy fell asleep believing his cock would burn a hole in the mattress.

He woke again a little later, but kept his face in the pillow. A quarrel was going on. Apparently the Cardinal had tried to get one of the Lady Birds to put on a fancy dress, and she was now outraged. She refused to calm down, and John Anthony was buying her off with what sounded like an umbrella. Tommy fell asleep again.

He next woke to music, and knew at once what to expect. Papageno's arias were coming from the tape recorder. The one playing as he woke was "Ein Mädchen oder Weibchen" and John Anthony, who loved Rilke above all other poets, was singing along in a perfect German accent.

Tommy turned over in spite of himself.

"Sorry. Didn't mean to wake you," said John Anthony. He was crawling around on the floor, wearing nothing but his hairy wax-paper skin. "I had a minute, so I thought I'd come in for a change of clothes. Should I get something for you too?"

"Don't bother. I'll change later."

Tommy waited. It took a little longer than usual, but it came.

"Look at this, will you? Just look what I've found!" cried John Anthony, rising.

He held in his hands a gorgeous green rag, a shimmering thing of chiffon and sequins. Tommy couldn't tell what it was until John Anthony had pulled it on. It was a little strapless ballet dress. The skirt ended about half-way down John Anthony's meaty genitals.

"What kind of face would go with this?" John Anthony wondered.

Tommy steeled himself as John Anthony searched the walls. Dear God, let him take one from somewhere else for a change!

John Anthony approached the cot. The mask he wanted happened to be on the wall above Tommy. He leaned over, and Tommy closed his eyes and breathed through his mouth as the balls flipped and flopped above him.

"Excuse," said John Anthony with no expression in his voice.

In the ballerina frock and in a face that looked like Albert Einstein, but doggier, John Anthony danced for Tommy. It was quite a while before Tommy could go to sleep again.

He was awakened by a pimpled youth with a long black beard. Tommy took a bowl of watery red soup that he knew would taste exactly as the Aviary dining room smelled—of fried onions, cold lamb drippings, dirty feet and garbage. He sipped some to be polite. Should I grow a beard? he asked himself, studying the boy who was staring into space. Tommy never shaved any more, but instead cut the hair down with scissors once a week. The heavy growth hid his face a little, and certainly a beard would hide it even more. But wasn't it sinful to hide it? Wasn't a beard a disguise, a mask?

He drank about a third of the soup and then gave the bowl back to the boy who took it with a contemptuous look. Without a word, the boy drank down the rest of the soup before leaving the attic.

Music woke him once again. Madrigals. Ah, madrigals! How Tommy loved them. The room was growing dark, but John Anthony sat humming at his worktable. Though he didn't look to see if Tommy was awake, he talked to him occasionally. He began a dirty joke but lost the point. Tommy felt happy and drifted in and out of sleep. He felt safe. Night was coming. Soon he would be out in the city again, wandering abandoned streets where he belonged.

"You could be one of us," John Anthony said suddenly. "You could stay here with us and we could take care of you."

"Aren't I already one of you?" Tommy replied.

33

Tommy thanked God as he paid his quarter and entered the jeweled and fragrant darkness. The theater was almost empty but the film had already begun—a cowboy picture as usual. With a spectacular dawn tossed casually over his shoulder, the lone rider, Randolph Scott, was dismounting beside a noisy blue river. Oh, God was good! God was generous! Out of the desert rocks He made crystal waters flow. Through the plains of hot sand He pushed fields of wild orange daisies.

His exalted heart shouting Halleluiah, Tommy went down the aisle to his special row, and then along the row to his special seat against the wall. He sprawled himself out, closed his eyes and fell asleep with heaven's glorious colors flickering over his eyelids. He dreamt he was lying inside a bouquet of immense roses.

Someone was groping him. He woke but kept his eyes closed, and when the hot heavy fingers slipped into his fly he gave a little snore to show that nothing could wake him. Mmmm, that felt nice. Who could it be? he wondered. Someone new? Whoever it was, he knew his business, and Tommy found it hard to keep from wriggling with delight. Whoever it was, Tommy loved him, and would have groped him back—longed to, in fact —but as always, he felt that if he woke, he would have to introduce his face. Sleeping, or even pretending to, he had no face. He was only his brightly burning cock.

The man leaned over and began to blow him. Tommy opened his eyes and looked down at the back of the head, but didn't recognize it. Ah yes, whoever it was, he knew what he was up to. What a palatial throat! Tommy couldn't prevent his buttocks from twitching, and the man, patting him on the knee, sucked more greedily. Tommy snored. He even snored as he came, and loudly, to cover up the snorts.

He felt good afterwards, though sticky, and went happily back among his roses which were now full of sap.

A woman was staring at him. Her huge face, with its huge shocked eyes, rode through the dark, coming closer and closer. Tommy threw his hands up in front of him to hide his shame. When he peered out between his fingers, he saw that he was in a richly furnished room, and that he was spoiling the wealth and the beauty of three beautiful people. Two men and the woman who had stared at him.

Screwing up his eyes, he screamed, "Forgive me! Forgive me!"

Though the Comet was crowded by now, no one in the audience paid any attention to Tommy's cries. They were used to hysterical queens and delirious bums.

"Tommy . . . My Tommy . . ."

A hand was playing up the back of his neck, into his hair.

"Oh, Tommy, my own, my love, my own true love . . ."

He kept his eyes closed.

"I'll never let you go again. Never, never."

No. Oh, dear God, no! No no no no no.

He sprang out of his seat and over Ismael's knees, crushing toes, kicking shins, as he stumbled, stumbled forever, out of his special row. He raced up the aisle and banged the doors open. In the blazing afternoon light he ran while the wolves snapped at his face and wolves snapped at his heels.

34

I am lovely. I am a tall mimosa tree exploding with blossoms. The wind gathers me up in its hands and we fly across the city, enchanting the dreary and the forlorn. I am Technicolor movies sprinkling rainbows over the drab streets. I am Marilyn Monroe and Tony Curtis rolled into one. Except that she is dead and that he has lost his looks.

Xavier strode along the Bowery in the cold hard sunlight. His eyes were big and almost purple, as were his earmuffs. He had a short thin blond beard and his hair reached nearly to his shoulders and also rose in waves above his head. Deep inside him, like an ecstatic lark in a mimosa tree, his heart sang. For it was morning and cold and full of sun. And he was free.

An old bum with a bloated scabby face and an out-stretched hand came out of a doorway. Xavier reached into his pocket and, finding two nickels, gave one to the bum.

"One for you and one for me. Fair's fair," he said, feeling guilty.

The bum flung his arms around Xavier. "There's my honey boy, my golden darling. Honey boy, let me tell you a little secret."

Lifting his right earmuff, Xavier inclined his head. The cold lips kissed his ear and the dry crusty tongue licked him.

Xavier giggled, breaking away.

"Ah, the darling," said the bum.

35

Loping through the wet and glistening night, Xavier
felt free. The night was hung with sourceless lights—
red and green and gas-blue smudges in the slick air.
Headlights occasionally boomed through the rain, tires
crackled over the asphalt, windshield wipers marched
like troops. It was too much, and too beautiful. The
night threw its arms around Xavier and hugged him till
he gasped.

The streets around Union Square were empty. The
trees were bare. Xavier's hair was plastered down in
large dark curls and his beard dripped. His soaked earmuffs spat cold sharp shots into his ears. He thought he
would probably die of pneumonia before dawn, but it
didn't matter, because he was free. A poem about the

night and the rain and the lights formed in his head. Suddenly, with an exultant cry of joy and freedom, he sprang into the air, touching a cold branch overhead. The tree unloaded its water on him.

Shivering, he hurried down Fourteenth Street and went into the Automat. Warm and steamy, like diving into a bowl of vegetable soup. His teeth chattered as his grateful body learned of the heat.

Xavier looked around at the people and saw that they were the ones, or just like the ones, who crowded into Union Square on fair nights. There were the old men and women who looked Jewish and sounded like books about the 1930's. Even here in the Automat, he could hear them quarreling about Roosevelt and Franco and Hitler and Stalin. The New Deal. ILGWU. NRA. WPA. CP. The initials floated around like the letters in alphabet soup.

There were also cab drivers and truck drivers having their midnight lunches, students, bums, and one table in the middle was packed with Latin American queens who were carrying on like ladies in evening gowns drinking champagne at an uptown club. And there were some solitaries—inexplicable people who sat, refusing to explain themselves. They caught Xavier's imagination. He thought of them, as he did of himself, as night creatures.

The most interesting night creature around at the moment was a man with a twisted face who was sitting alone beside the window. Xavier bought himself a cup of coffee and carried it over to the table.

"May I?" he asked, startling Tommy who was looking out the window.

"What?"

"Can I sit down here?"

Tommy nodded vaguely. It was really more of a shrug than a nod, but Xavier took it to mean welcome.

He sat down and sweetened his coffee. Across the street a chauffered limousine pulled up outside Luchow's. Xavier glanced at Tommy and saw that he too was looking at the car.

"Is that a nightclub?" he asked.

"Luchow's? No, it's a res—" Tommy flushed, believing it was ridiculous that a face like his should know what went on across the street. "I've heard it's a restaurant." He hoped the boy wouldn't talk to him again.

Xavier sipped his coffee and made a face, but Tommy didn't notice. Xavier sipped again, slurping this time and letting his teeth chatter against the cup. Tommy was looking out the window.

"This coffee tastes funny," Xavier lied. "A little salty. I bet some joker mixed salt up in the sugar shaker. Did yours taste funny?"

"No," Tommy said, without moving his eyes. He was sure the boy was making fun of him.

Xavier felt like an idiot. He blushed and looked out the window. The limousine was driving away. The street was empty again. It was pouring rain except under Luchow's awning. Luchow. Hmmm. Maybe they could talk about Luchow's. "Chinese, I suppose," he said, turning to Tommy with a smile.

Tommy neither moved nor spoke, but such a look of horror came into his eyes that Xavier immediately looked out at the street again. What had the man seen? There was only the rain, not a soul was passing. Yet, obviously, the man had seen something horrible. Where was it? Who was it?

Though he wanted to run from the table, Tommy couldn't move. He sat staring at the rain, paralyzed by anguish. He couldn't even blink. He wanted the moment to pass. He wanted it never to have happened.

Finally, though still caught in the boy's eyes as in quicksand, Tommy began to pull himself free. An arm out, then a leg. He pushed his chair back. He lifted himself to his feet. And then he bolted forward and went through the doors.

36

Now that Mary had the key to the private park where the weather was always fine and the trees were always green, Johnson the guard never failed to lift his cap and say a few kind words when she wheeled Emilio in his grand white carriage through the gates. And she was so grateful for his attentions that tears came into her eyes. For, alas, no one else in the gardens was the least bit friendly to her. They were hardly even civil. All those wives and nursemaids sunning themselves on the grass or pushing their carriages along the shady lanes— they treated Mary as if she stank.

"Good afternoon" was the most they would say, all but holding their noses as she passed.

Mary felt lonely. She'd never felt so lonely before in

her life. In spite of her twelfth-floor terrace apartment looking over the park. In spite of her clothes and her money. In spite of Emily. Dear dear Emily. No girl could have hoped for a more generous and loving husband, a more devoted father for her child. But Emily was at the office all day, and when she came home, well —she was the pipe and slippers sort. The newspaper, a couple of bottles of cold beer, peek-a-boo with Emilio, TV, a hearty supper, and bed. Or sometimes bed and then supper. She wasn't one for giggles and gossip like the ladies out in the park.

Besides, what was the point of being rich if everybody treated you the same as they had when you were poor? An outcast again. Lonely and unloved. Mary lay awake all night tossing and suffering. "I was born Mary Poorpoor and I'll die Mary Poorpoor," she told herself, shedding tears. Quiet tears so as not to wake Emily. And why, dear God in heaven, why? Just because she didn't have a nice big empty carriage like the rest of the ladies. Her carriage had to be full of Emilio! Oh no, she wasn't going to put up with it much longer. Oh no, she wasn't. If the rules of the game meant an empty carriage, then an empty carriage Mary was going to have.

So after lunch one day, instead of dressing Emilio, she threw him into his rocking-horse cradle and dissolved a Miltown in his bottle. As he suckled, he looked up at her, an eyebrow raised, a sly crooked grin at his lips. He knew what she was up to, that was clear, and she felt like kicking him. Probably he was already planning how he would get even with her. But she didn't care. Life was too short to worry about consequences.

Mary took the elevator down to the basement and rolled her empty carriage up the ramp.

"Good afternoon, Miss Mary," said Johnson as she came through the iron gates. "And how is little Emilio today?"

"Just as fine as fine can be." She was nervous in spite of herself, and she blushed when Johnson peered under the hood.

The guard, however, was perfectly composed. "You surely have the cutest baby in the park," he said, looking squarely into Mary's eyes.

"I think so myself." With a triumphant smile, she began to walk on. "Though, of course, I'm prejudiced."

She followed the path to the goldfish pond in the poplar grove because just beyond it was a stretch of lawn where a certain half-dozen ladies always sat. Each afternoon they left their carriages in the shade around the pond, but they sat within earshot in case their invisible babies cried. They were very good mothers and never stopped running over to fuss with their carriages.

These were Mary's favorite ladies. They were the most terrific snobs in the park and had invariably ignored her completely, never greeting nor even noticing her when she passed. Mary knew them not only by sight but by name, for she'd often heard Johnson greet them. But only one name mattered. Mrs. Abbeyberg. Harriet Abbeyberg. She was the star. You could tell that in a single glance. None of the other ladies ever really talked to each other; they all talked to Mrs. Abbeyberg. She was the only one who mattered. With her tight white jeans, her tight black sleeveless sweater, her long loose auburn hair, Mrs. Abbeyberg was the star. She was such a star that she didn't even bother shaving her armpits.

Mary wheeled her carriage across a corner of the lawn, just the way she usually did, as if taking a short cut. But this time she cut the corner rather wide, and when she was only a couple of yards from the ladies, who were passing a thermos bottle around, she stopped suddenly and braked the wheels.

"Dear, oh dear," she exclaimed and leaned under the hood, knowing that the ladies had their eyes on her. Very slowly and very elaborately, she lifted the baby up into her arms. "Sh-sh, hush, my darling." While she rocked him at her bosom, she turned to Mrs. Abbeyberg and smiled apologetically. "His teeth. Just awful!"

Mrs. Abbeyberg's eyebrows lifted in surprise, and for a moment her long horsy face remained frozen. Oh that terrible hateful woman, thought Mary, wishing the earth would open and swallow all of them. She felt like such an idiot standing there hushing and rocking a baby that didn't exist. She felt as though she had laid the most gigantic fart, and the ladies were just going to sit and wait patiently until both it and Mary dissolved in the breeze. She almost grabbed her carriage and ran, but then she caught the slightest shadow of a twitch at Mrs. Abbeyberg's mouth.

All at once, all the ladies threw up their hands, nodded their heads and rolled their eyes in sympathy. They all understood the horrors of teething!

And in the very next moment, the six marvelous women jumped to their feet and surrounded Mary, offering her advice, hugging her in sympathy, tickling little

What's his name?

Emilio.

Come sit down with us.

Why thank you.

There's vodka martini in the thermos. Help yourself.

Why thank you thank you thank you thank you.

37

On Thursday afternoons between three and five, each of the ladies in turn threw a cocktail party. Today was Mary's first turn as hostess, and she'd been up and around since six in the morning. Emily teased her during breakfast but gave her a little extra money to top up the liquor cabinet.

"Just keep calm, and everything will go fine," Emily told her. "And don't get so excited that you forget about your son."

As soon as Emily was gone, Mary rearranged the terrace. Emily liked to have it looking like a jungle, with the potted palm, lemon and banana trees spread across the breadth of it. That wasn't the way Mrs. Abbeyberg did things. So Mary pushed all the trees over on the left.

They looked more like a jungle than ever, but smaller, and there was now much more space for the party.

Aside from the cocktails, the girls usually served something unexpected and, if possible, silly. Like chocolate cookies or canapés of spinach mashed with peanut butter. To be safe as well as silly Mary decided to serve Russian caviar on slices of raw potato. Also to be safe, she bought two new canvas chairs, making a total of ten on her terrace, or three more than she actually needed. Like Mrs. Abbeyberg, she leaned the three spares against the parapet.

Everything was ready in plenty of time. Everything except Emilio. Mary couldn't figure out what to do about him. It was customary for the ladies to bring along their children on Thursdays and lay them out around the hostess's nursery. So where could she put Emilio? You had to go through the living room to get to the terrace, and the dining area didn't have a door. You had to pass through the master bedroom to reach the toilet, and Mrs. Abbeyberg might want to pee. Should she stash him in a closet? But babies often suffocated in closets, not that Mary cared. She loved her invisible baby a thousand times more than this one. Emily, however, would object if he died, might never forgive her.

So then where? Heavens, it was already three o'clock! She dropped a Nembutal into his bottle and walked around the house with him in her arms while he drank. Where? The laundry bin? The refrigerator? Under the bed? He might roll out. Disgusted, she looked down at him, expecting—but he was already asleep, and he hadn't drunk a third of the bottle. Maybe the pill had killed him. She put an ear against his heart.

The doorbell rang.

"Coming," she screamed.

Dear pretty God, what could she do with him? She ran into the kitchen and opened the door on the servants' stairway. The landing was dark but not *that* dark, and someone coming up the stairs would see him. She wished she could just wear him in her hair like an Easter bonnet. The doorbell rang.

Well, she would have to take a chance. Quick as a flash, she slid the iron turkey roaster from under the kitchen sink, stuck Emilio into it and laid it just outside the door. She put the lid on at an angle, so that he could breathe. But what if some delivery boy looked inside the pot—or stole it? Don't think about that. She locked the door and stuck the key in her brassiere.

The bell rang again and this time didn't stop until Mary went to the door.

"What happened, did you fall in?" Mrs. Abbeyberg asked.

"No. Oh, you know, Emilio again."

"You mean that runny nose? How is he?"

Mary led the ladies into the nursery so they could see for themselves. They found him looking a lot better than he had the last few days. Mary was just too anxious a mother, they said. It would show on him when he grew up. You know what boys with overprotective mothers turn out to be!

They laid their babies down. Two in the playpen, one into the cradle with Emilio, two on the sitter's cot, and one in the wing chair near the door.

"Someone tell me when it's four o'clock," said Mrs. Abbeyberg. "Did you ever see the size of these suppositories? Stick a few hairs on the end and it's sexual intercourse."

Mary then took the ladies on a tour of the apartment, and they all remarked how interesting it was, though perhaps a bit Victorian.

"Emily likes things that are solid and substantial," Mary wretchedly explained.

After that, the liquor trolley was wheeled out on the terrace, and the party began.

". . . eight, nine, ten," Mrs. Abbeyberg said, counting the chairs. She then took a canapé, flicking off the caviar with her finger and eating just the raw potato. I'm hopelessly old-fashioned, Mary thought.

But the party was a success. The ladies drank and drank and drank, and the talk got dirtier and dirtier. They talked about how big their husbands' cocks were, how long they could fuck without coming, and how much gism they could shoot. Presently they got on the subject of abortions. All the ladies had had a few. Except Mary, but she went along with the conversation, not really saying anything, but agreeing rather loudly.

When the stories were becoming bloodier and more detailed, the doorbell rang. Mary was suddenly busy refreshing drinks.

"Harriet dear, would you see who that is?" she called. She felt very proud that whoever it was would see Mrs. Abbeyberg opening Mary's door like an old friend.

While Mrs. Abbeyberg was away, the ladies fell silent, having no one to talk to. They clinked the ice in their glasses, stretched their legs, scratched their cunts, lit cigarettes. It was like an intermission.

Mrs. Abbeyberg returned from the door alone and with a very odd smile on her face.

"Who was it?" Mary asked.

"No one."

"No one? That's funny. I thought I heard a ring."

"Maybe so, but when I got to the door there was no one."

"Oh," said Mary. What a peculiar smile! It looked somehow familiar. Hmmm.

The party was in the doldrums and it was only half-past four. Mrs. Abbeyberg gave no sign whether it would be smarter to continue telling abortion stories or to go on to something new. The intermission seemed endless. Mary was beginning to feel her party was a failure.

Then Mrs. Abbeyburg turned to her.

She said, "I'll bet you've had your share of gruesome abortions too. Am I right, Mary?"

"Heaps. Dozens."

"Tell me about them." She still had that funny smile. In fact all the ladies had them now.

"Well, let me think," Mary began. "I suppose the most interesting abortion I ever had was the last one—

just a few months ago. The whole thing was a terrible mistake from beginning to end. First of all, I waited until I was in my fourth month before I did anything about it. Don't tell me I'm crazy, I know I am." She crossed her eyes to be funny. The ladies smiled.

"But it's just as you were all saying, what with the Cuban revolution and that man in Pennsylvania arrested, where was I to go? I'd heard about the doctor in Harlem of course, but . . . well . . . you know . . .

"Anyway. I finally found someone in New York, just off Columbus Circle. Maybe it's the same one you were talking about before, Harriet—the one on Fifty-eighth Street?"

Mrs. Abbeyberg said nothing, but she smiled and moved her head. Over her shoulder, through the terrace doors, Mary saw something move on the living-room floor. For one wild moment, she thought it must be one of the invisible babies. But then, her heart sinking, she saw who it was.

The ladies had all followed her eyes, and now they turned to her. "What's the matter, Mary? Is anything wrong?"

"Wrong? What could be wrong? Where was I, anyway? Oh, that guy on Fifty-ninth Street. Well, he wouldn't take care of me because I made the mistake of telling him how far gone I was. After that—let me think . . ." Could she pretend to start sweeping in the middle of her story? That was a little rude, but he was heading toward the terrace now.

"Yes, Emily found someone for me. That's what it

was. I can't remember how. He was an old German who lived in the Bronx."

"Not old Schisselmann?" cried the ladies.

"Y—" Mary caught herself in time. Perhaps it was a trick question. "No, something like that. I really can't remember. You'd have to ask Emily. Anyhoo, he did the abortion on his dining-room table. You know, those big old-fashioned dining-room sets? Well, that kind of table." The ladies smiled. She supposed they were thinking of her table. "He laid a plastic tablecloth out under me. And that's about all I remember of the actual operation because I fainted dead away. The really bad part comes later."

He was out on the terrace now, but crawling left toward the trees. Maybe he'd get lost among them until the ladies left.

"Mary!" the ladies said. "Have you fallen asleep?"

"No, I haven't. I'm a slow thinker. The next part of the story belongs to Emily. You see, that German had told her to come and call for me at eight o'clock in the evening. She was there on time naturally, and later she told me that when he took her into the bedroom where I was sleeping, she thought for sure I was dead. She said I was white as a sheet and lay all flopped out like a rag doll. She couldn't even feel a pulse or hear a heartbeat. Can you imagine?

" 'What's wrong with her?' she screamed.

"And that butcher said, 'Don't vorry, mein dear. Dere's nutting to vorry about. Ve had a tiny tiny bit of unexpected trrroubles. It was a very big baby, you see.

The biggest I ever delivered, so to speak. A boy. You were very naughty not to tell me how advanced the pregnancy was. So we had to take him out bit by bit.' "

He was in among the trees now, and Mary heaved a sigh of relief. Just stay there, she prayed. Just stay there.

"So Emily said, 'Bit by bit or all at once, what difference does that make? Why does Mary look like this?'

" 'Dere isn't anything to vorry about. She'll be perfectly fine as soon as de rest comes out.'

"Imagine hearing that! 'The rest? You mean you've left part of the baby inside?'

" 'Nein nein, aber nein. Just the head. Und not even really all of that. Bud mein dear lady, vat can you expect? She vas probably already in de sixt mont. But dere's nutting to vorry about. Nature vill take care of everything, even in matters like this. Nature is no moralist. She never judges. She merely acts. Your little darling is safe in nature's hands. In a day or two at the most, the little head vill pop out all by itself.' "

Of course Emilio had been listening, for on the last line his head appeared above the lemon trees nearest the parapet. He must have crawled up the slender trunks like a monkey. And he was grinning at her!

So were the ladies. "Mary . . . You hoo . . ." they said.

"Emily wasn't very reassured, but what could she do except wait? So she let the butcher send her home.

"In the middle of the night, I finally woke up. I don't know what time it was, but I woke with the worst pains

I ever had before or since, knock wood. Terrible terrible pains. And funny ones, because I thought, pardon me, that what was wrong was that I had to move my bowels."

The lemon tree leaned over and Emilio crawled across the branches and sat down on the parapet. He had a very broad smile now, broad and almost innocent. Dear God, don't let him fall. Emily will never forgive me.

"Mary, Mary, quite contrary!" said the ladies. "What a storyteller you are!"

"There really isn't much more to tell. As I said, I thought I had to go to the bathroom. So I crawled out of bed. It was dark in the room and it didn't occur to me to look for a light. I just sort of wandered around dizzily. And then I saw a bucket under a small washstand in the corner." He was right at the edge of the parapet now. What should she do? What should she do? "You can bet your life I headed straight for that bucket. I sat down and gave a little squeeze and kerplunk! Gracious, what a turd, I thought, but I didn't—"

Suddenly, with a slight jerk of his arms, Emilio was over and on the way down. She heard him cry Mama as he fell through the air. Mary nearly rose in her chair. My baby, my baby, her broken heart wailed after him.

"—I didn't look to see what it was. On the way out it felt as big as a melon or one of those tin globes of the world. Anyway, as soon as it dropped out I felt better. I went straight to sleep again and in the morning Emily came and woke me up and took me home. And, *voilà*, here I am!"

The ladies applauded. They didn't have their funny smile any more. "You win," they said. "You win hands down. That's the most gruesome abortion story I've ever heard."

Five o'clock. Time to go. The ladies gathered up their babies, chucked Emilio under the chin, and said their goodbyes.

Mary took her invisible Emilio up in her arms and wandered miserably around the apartment. What would Emily say when she came home? Would she accept the new baby as her own? Mary unlocked the door on the servants' stairway and dragged the roaster in. How'd the little devil ever get out? And how did he get back in?

"Good Lord!" she gasped. "I haven't bought Emily's supper!"

Grabbing her shopping bag, she rode down the twelve flights to the street. There he was, out on the walk in front of the house! A pile of bloody meat! It made her shudder. Death, how awful and tragic! The pavement was covered with bloody footsteps and carriage tracks. The ladies had passed right through the mess.

What oh what would Emily think? She would never never forgive Mary. Life in the enchanted garden was as good as over. With endless sighs and tears, Mary went into the local supermarket and pulled things off the shelves for supper. For her Last Supper! Life was such hell! London broil. Artichoke hearts. Ice cream. Olives stuffed with capers. Frozen bisque of lobster. And a whole terrace smeared with caviar.

38

c/o Poste Restante
Bongoville, Africa

Dear Dr. Franzblau,

Once, long long ago, I wrote you another letter. Maybe you remember me—Isobel, the Yellow Rose. I was just a baby then and I had no idea how really cruel and cunning Fate could be. Why didn't I listen to the good advice you gave me in your column? But I never did call up the Community Guidance Service. I thought I was too smart for psychoanalysis. If only I'd listened to you, maybe I'd finally have adjusted to Tommy's looks and married him. Maybe I'd have a bunch of kids by now and be somewhere civilized instead of hiding out in this jungle.

But no! I was too smart. Or maybe you would say I was too much of a coward to stay and face my problems. I ran away from them, Dr. Franzblau. I left Tommy God knows where. I abandoned my poor widowed mother and all my little brothers and sisters. And where have I ended up?

The nearest town isn't more than a village, built out of mud and dung, with a few skyscrapers that the French left. Please cut your column about me out when it is published and send it to me here in Bongoville, c/o Poste Restante, as I mention above. But I guess I should tell you frankly that I know the town pretty well now and there is no Community Guidance or any other psychological service. Except an old man who runs a souvenir shop. He's a kind of witch doctor. If you think I should see him I will, but I don't believe he's what I need.

I am writing this by candlelight in a tiny thatched hut made out of driftwood and flotsam on the wildest, jungliest coast of Africa. My house has no floor, just the ground and the straw mat I sleep on. I can hear the waves banging on the beach, but they don't make things any cooler. It is hot hot hot. The sweat is dripping from me. It is full of ticks here, as big as rats, and mosquitoes and fleas and every other bug you can imagine, crawling and flying. The ants have teeth just like German Shepherds. I don't know how I manage to keep a drop of blood in my veins. But it's better here than right in Bongoville which is full of real rats and diseases.

You are probably wondering how I happen to be so far from home. Well, the answer is simple. I am in hiding because someone is pursuing me. Someone wants to kill me!! And it's not my imagination, Dr. Franzblau. He's as real as you and me, and he's after my throat.

You see, when I ran away from New York on account of Tommy I began a life of—should I call it travel? Or should I tell the truth and call it—Sin? Yes, sin! I went all over the States selling myself like a common whore, like a prostitute. And when I finally got disgusted, I went to Europe. And what did I do there? Sell myself like a whore, like a common prostitute. I settled down in Amsterdam on the Achtburgwal. You know, I guess, that street on the canal where the girls all sit in the windows like shop dummies.

I was one of those girls. And I was also the most successful because I am very dark and beautiful. Or *was*. And I had a lot of charm too. I could be particular. I didn't have to take on just any old comer. You should have seen the number of men I turned down every night. They'd hang around in the shadows under the trees along the canal looking at me in my window and whacking themselves off. The girls used to call that window-shopping.

I had a lot of offers of marriage, sometimes from guys who were handsome and rich. But I always refused. Why? God knows. Maybe I have a block against marriage because I feel guilt over Tommy. It's possible.

Anyway, I had one suitor who was more persistent

than the rest, and more determined. He was a sailor, a merchant seaman. He was the cutest sweetest thing you ever saw, and probably sexy if you dig boys which I don't and never really have. I like men. But Dickie was cuddly and adorable. I always let him in free. He had five days shore leave every two months, being on a run between Rotterdam and Veracruz. And he always stayed with me those five days. I even fed him, and never took a single a penny from him, only gifts which I couldn't stop him from buying. I said, Dickie, if you have extra money to burn, send it to my mother. I have never forgotten Mama or the kids.

Dickie proposed to me every two months, five days running, night and day. I used to just laugh and say, Go on. I knew this bothered him, but I couldn't have dreamed how much. He would say I turned him down because he was poor. And this was not the truth. Perhaps there is something in my psyche that just won't let me find joy or peace. Maybe you can understand that, Dr. Franzblau.

One day Dickie's ship came in in more ways than one. He rushed over to the Achtburgwal and took me into his boyish arms. He said, "I'm not poor any more, Isobel." And he whipped his duffel bag or whatever you call it and pulled out more pearls than I'd ever seen before in my life. Real pearls. Three strands of them. Maybe 200 pearls altogether.

He stole them from some rich married woman in New York who was in love with him. I could see they were worth a fortune; 100 G's was the price he expected to get from the fence in Rio.

"You did this for me, Dickie," I said and burst into tears. I couldn't help it, I was so touched. This boy who was such an angel and so good, who never so much as harmed a fly in all his life—he turned into a criminal and all because of me. For my love.

I said, "You should never have done this."

He said, "I'll do worse than this if you don't marry me. I'm desperate for you, Isobel, desperate. You don't know how much you mean to me."

And I a girl from the Achtburgwal!

But Dickie was wrong. I knew now how much I meant to him. And I realized then that I had come to love him in spite of myself.

I said, "All right, darling. I will marry you."

The plan was for him to ship out as usual at the end of the five days and to leave the pearls with me. I was supposed to wait one month and then catch a plane to Rio and go to the Hotel Majestic. Dickie would jump ship at Veracruz and meet me in Rio. Then we'd get rid of the pearls and get married and live happily ever after.

Happily ever after! As if such a thing were possible for me. As if I

I heard a sound out in the jungle just now. Probably just a panther or a snake. Every time I hear a sound, Dr. Franzblau, I practically jump out of my skin. I think it must be Dickie. He's found me at last and he'll never give me a chance to explain. He'll just grab me and slit my guts open. He'll never believe it was panic that made me run away.

Where was I anyway? Still in Amsterdam. Well, it was my job to do the smuggling. Dickie was really smart. That's what worries me. He still is. He's found out every hiding place I've stuck myself into. His idea was that I should dress up in a lot of flashy clothes, really vulgar. Earrings, bracelets, rings, the works, all obvious junky stuff. Put on lots of makeup. A cheap monkey-skin collar. And then to wear the pearls right out in the open.

And that's what I did. I probably looked like a Gypsy or some kind of slut, but I got through Dutch customs without anyone batting an eye. On the plane, though, I started getting nervous on account of the hostess. She kept looking at me in a funny way. Looking at my clothes, my hair, my face, and then at the pearls, like the whole thing didn't go together. A couple of times she came by with the pilot or somebody, some guy in uniform, and they both gave me these weird looks. I got scared.

So when they passed the supper trays out I made believe I was sick. I made a lot of noise, and the old lady next to me got all upset and called the hostess. I made a lot of faces and horrible noises like I was vomiting, and finally they helped me to the toilet. Half the passengers had stopped eating by this time on account of my noises. As soon as I was inside the toilet, I locked the door. I stayed inside probably for half an hour, and I ate every last one of those pearls, string, latch and all.

The hostess kept knocking and saying, "Are you all right there, honey? Please let me in."

Not on your life!

I bet I came out of the can looking worse than when I went in. She helped me up the aisle to my seat, and I swear, Dr. Franzblau, I could hear those pearls rattling inside me. I felt like I had three pounds of marbles in my belly. I asked the hostess for a couple of Cokes as I thought this might get the air out of me and settle the pearls together. And maybe the whole thing is the Coke's fault, as I've heard even teeth dissolve in it. The hostess also gave me a sleeping pill. But before I fell asleep, she realized about my necklace.

She said, "Those beautiful pearls. Did you take them off?"

I touched my throat and acted surprised. "I don't know. I'm sure I had them on when I went into the ladies' room. And I don't remember taking them off."

She got all excited and ran off to the toilet. When she came back she was as nervous as a wet hen. Because she didn't find the pearls, see.

But by now I was feeling dopey and nice, and the pearls weren't bothering me. I thought, Up yours, sister. I said, "Just cool it, honey. Maybe they fell in the bowl when I puked and they dropped into space and they're at the bottom of the Atlantic Ocean by this time. But don't worry about it. They weren't worth more than a grand."

She laughed. What else could she do?

In the morning I felt great and

I swear there's something going on outside. Maybe it's just that gorilla that hangs around like one of those window-shoppers.

So I got through customs right as rain, and I grabbed a cab and went straight to the Majestic. My mistake was that I didn't register under my own name. I was still a little scared, see. If I'd registered under my own name, at least I'd be able to prove to Dickie I meant to meet him and wasn't just trying to double-cross him with the fence.

I called up the room service and ordered a bottle of castor oil. I drank most of a pint and went into my bathroom and on the plugged bidet. To catch it. I didn't have to wait long, but a lot came out before the pearls arrived. Actually they wouldn't come out by themselves. They were sort of stuck. I had to reach under and in, and pull. And pull and pull and pull. Three strands, remember. It felt so disgusting and was so disgusting that I kept my eyes closed the whole time and breathed through my mouth. When I got them all out I threw them into the sink and let the tap run a long long time before I looked.

And what did I see when I looked? The worst surprise of my life. They weren't the same pearls as the ones I swallowed in the airplane. They'd turned into three strands of little brown broken things. Like a necklace of rotten baby teeth.

I digested them is what happened, and I'm enclosing a photo so you can see for yourself that I'm telling the truth. I GLOW, Dr. Franzblau. I really and truly

GLOW. But that didn't start happening until weeks later.

By that time I was running for my life. From Rio to Lima to Panama to Mexico City. To New York. Back to Europe. I stopped in each city just long enough to pick up my fare to the next. I've heard from whores

39

"It needs a touch more glue at the left ear," John Anthony said, dabbing Tommy's temples with the sponge. "But we'll have to wait a minute, my back hurts from bending over. I've had lumbago ever since my Paris days. If I bend over for too long a time it starts hurting again. Right here," he added turning around. "Just above my asphodels."

Wincing, he limped across the room to the cot and lay down on his belly.

Tommy, who was sitting on the stool beside the worktable, looked out the window at the red brick wall on the other side of the courtyard. There was a little bit of sky to see as well, a ribbon of smoky gray just above the wall.

"Is it very hot in there?" John Anthony asked.

"It doesn't matter," Tommy said. "It feels just the same as my face."

"Well, you dont have to pout. It doesn't look the same." John Anthony groaned and punched himself in the kidneys with his fists.

"I'm not pouting," said Tommy apologetically. Did it really feel the same as his face? From inside it felt as if he were locked in an Iron Maiden. And from outside? He hesitated, then touched it, his fingers springing away in horror. It felt like a snake.

"You shouldn't touch it," said John Anthony. "That takes away the illusion. At least, you shouldn't until you get used to it."

After a while, in a very soft voice, Tommy asked, "Isn't this a sin, John Anthony?"

"A sin?" he repeated, shocked. "You mean the mask?"

"I mean concealing what God did to me. I mean hiding His madness."

"Nothing you do for love can be a sin, my dear. The Archbishop of Milan once said so himself."

"Oh," said Tommy coldly. Through the holes in his mask, he looked out of the window again. "My eyeballs feel naked. Maybe I should get myself a pair of glasses, so then all my face will be covered."

Because of the lumbago, John Anthony had to get off the bed ass-backwards and then kneel on the floor before straightening himself up slowly. When he could walk, he went to the bassinet and picked up the hand-mirror.

"Look!" he said. "Look at Tommy brought back to life."

Tommy shut his eyes and pushed the mirror away. "No, I don't want to see."

"Stop being such a baby. Come on, take a peek. You're very good to look at."

"I know what it looks like. I saw it before I put it on. I saw it all day yesterday."

"But that's not the same thing as now," said John Anthony, shoving the mirror at him again. "Because now it's alive."

Tommy shuddered. "Stop it! I won't look," he said. "I can't look in mirrors. I never have looked in mirrors—not since the day I went into the hospital."

"You mean you've never seen your face?"

Tommy shook his head. "I know how it looks though."

"No, you don't," John Anthony said, laying the mirror on his worktable. "It looks beautiful. It looked beautiful before and it looks beautiful now." And bending, he kissed Tommy on the lips.

40

When Tommy saw the silver Jaguar sitting at the curb, almost the same color as the dusk, the fear of God went out of him and he became afraid of Man instead.

He imagined the convertible belonged to a rival, an elegant East Side playboy with a French haircut and tight clothes. He saw the big white teeth, the trim compact body, the long legs spinning in the air while Ismael humped over him, or— Who fucked whom, Tommy wondered in anguish, but since he couldn't bear the thought of anyone except himself plunging into Ismael, he put the question out of his mind.

A pastel shirt, pants so tight it looked like he had a cannon and a pair of cannon balls pressed against his left thigh, white tennis shoes, enormous shades with thin gold rims. The playboy. His life had never been interrupted by tumors, ugliness or poverty. The Jaguar just went tooling along speedways between all the fashionable cities on earth. He cut like a porpoise through a turquoise pool, with sharp abbreviated gestures. He hurried, eagerly. He swam in a hurry, eager for sun. He sunned himself in a hurry, eager for drinks. He drank in a hurry, eager for lunch. He ate in a hurry, eager for rest. He rested in a hurry, eager for—for rising cool as a cocktail sipped in the shade, to speed his way here and throw himself eagerly, eagerly, at Ismael's feet.

Miserable now, Tommy couldn't make himself climb the tenement stairs to face the playboy who even now was smiling his toothy maskless smile. Nor could he bring himself to turn around and go away. He stood on the walk in his old hat and coat and in his new face that looked just like his old face.

Little Luis came running out of the building. Tommy turned his face away, but the boy stopped next to him and stared. Gathering up his courage, Tommy met Luis' eyes. They were curious but showed no recognition.

"Hi," said Tommy, feeling good. "Whose little boy are you?"

"I'm Luis Rosa. Are you from Welfare?"

"No. I'm looking for Ismael Rosa. Is he related to you?"

"Who wants to know?"

"If Ismael is home, you can do me a favor and earn a little money."

"You can see for yourself he's home," Luis said, pointing at the Jaguar.

Tommy's heart sank. "Look," he said. He took a quarter out of his pocket and then, after hesitating, took his good luck penny from the band of his hat. "Go upstairs and tell Ismael that there's a man here who's got to talk to him about something special, and to come right down."

Luis took the money, nodded and dashed into the building. Tommy heard him run up the stairs, heard a door slam, and after a moment heard a window opening on an upper story. Feeling faint, Tommy went through the tenement door into the vestibule and leaned against the stamped tin wall. His face was scorching him and he pressed his masked cheek to the tin but wasn't cooled.

"He'll be right down," little Luis yelled, coming down the stairs.

Before he touched bottom Tommy was out in the street again.

"He'll be right down," Luis repeated.

"Thanks."

"He's putting on some clothes. He always wears a bikini around the house."

"I know," said Tommy without thinking.

But Luis didn't notice. "Could I have another dime? If you give me another dime I can go to the movies. I need thirty-five cents."

"I don't have any more money." He could hear Ismael's fast uneven footsteps, and his breath went.

"Come on, mister. One more dime won't kill you."

There was a smile on Ismael's face as he came through the door to the street. It vanished slowly.

"Are you the guy who wants to talk to me?" he asked.

Tommy's hands rose to his face. "Don't you know who I am?"

"No." He smiled again now, puzzled. "No, I don't think so. Should I?"

It was twilight, but it wasn't dark.

"Baby, it's me. It's Tommy." Under the mask his skin crawled, gasping for breath.

"Tommy? Are you kidding?"

"Look at me! Look at me! I've come back to you as I was because I love you."

With a scowl Ismael turned on little Luis. "Get your fuck ass outta here," he said and swiped at the boy with his hand.

Little Luis ran down the street.

Ismael said, "What kind of talk is that in front of a kid?"

"I don't care who hears me. I'll run down the street shouting it. I'm Tommy. I've come back. I love you."

Ismael folded his arms. He was wearing a blue T-shirt and clinging gunmetal pants. Spick whore, thought Tommy, hating him.

"Listen, mister, I don't know what your game is or what you want. But you're not Tommy." He shook his head slowly. "No, sir, you're not my Tommy."

"For God's sake, look at me!"

"I'm looking, man, I'm looking. And all I see is you, whoever you are."

Tears fell out of the holes in the mask. "I'm Tommy. I'm Tommy. I'm Tommy. I'm Tommy—" He closed his eyes, his heart breaking, his face burning.

"Listen, mister, I admit there's a resemblance to what Tommy *used* to look like. But my Tommy has a sweet crippled face now and a heart of gold. And I love him. I will as long as I live. He bought me that car there—a lot of shit you handsome guys ever buy anybody."

Ismael slid the keys from his pocket and shook them at Tommy's mask.

"Is that what you did with my money, with my life's savings, while I've been a bum on the Bowery?"

"Now, just you cool it, mister—"

"Stop calling me mister, you black slut," Tommy bellowed.

Ismael smiled and bared his gorgeous teeth. "I shit on you, mister. And I shit on you."

He walked past Tommy and leaped gracefully into the Jaguar. The grace of this leap enchanted Tommy, and then doubled his rage. But what could he do? He stood inside his mask while the motor idled and while Ismael narrowed his eyes with a lazy sexy look of pleasure.

"Be seeing you, mister," said Ismael, throwing the engine into gear.

As Tommy sprang toward Ismael, he meant to kill him. He meant to throw his hands around his strong brown throat and destroy him. But in mid-motion his intentions changed. His fingers flew at his own face, pinched and tore and pulled at it.

"What? What?" Ismael said, partly frightened, partly horrified.

The mask came off with a long loud ripping sound, and underneath it: the raw, red, boiled, baked, twisted flesh.

"My God! My God!" cried Ismael. "Oh my poor love."

Like an animal or a thunderstorm, Tommy roared wordlessly at Ismael, and thrust the mask on his face.

The smoke began to rise at once, and Ismael screamed. His hands went up to his face. The Jaguar bucked forward, but instead of stalling began bolting down the avenue like an unbroken bronco. Ismael's screams were lost among others. People were running. Bodies were falling. The car sprang and kicked along the twilit avenue, knocking over pushcarts, banging into fenders. Tommy saw billows of smoke rising from Ismael's head. He began running after the convertible.

Nearly two blocks away, the Jaguar finally jumped a curb, spun a full circle, and smashed into the wall of a tenement. When Tommy reached the wreck, a crowd had formed, but Ismael was still sitting at the wheel, his head wrapped in flames.

"Help me!" he cried. "Help me! Get me out of here!"

Tommy could see Ismael's huge green eyes as bright as emeralds glistening inside the red and yellow fire.

41

John Anthony locked the Aviary door, looked through it at the deserted street, yawned and felt a trembling in his limbs, switched off the downstairs lights and, in the dark, climbed to the top of the house and went into his room. Although the day had been long and hard, and his lids were heavy on his eyes, he sat down at his worktable and studied the seven new masks on which he'd lately been working. He was about to dip his brush into the pot of red ink when, hand raised in space, he sank into a dream of glory. He dreamt of the day his masks would line the walls of an uptown art gallery. He dreamt of being carried triumphantly on the shoulders of the rich and the celebrated into a world of brilliant lights and bubbles.

His hand fell, staining a forehead, and he woke, unbearably himself. His heart was a dark cave filled with sharp-toothed, fierce-clawed beasts that ran snapping and tearing through his blood. In pain he left the worktable and prowled around the room, singing to himself: Who can I be tonight? Who will I be tonight?

He closed his eyes and let his hands crawl out blindly. He touched things around him. Am I silk tonight, lace, velvet, serge, wool, flannel, burlap? His right hand tripped across a fabric full of shocks, thrilling his fingertips. He opened his eyes. The dress was orange satin covered with lace. It looked like veiled sherbet.

The touch and now the sight of it ended John Anthony's unhappiness. He stripped himself down and held the dress in front of him, his skin tingling. Hmmm. It was somewhat short, but above the knees was stylish now, so in spite of his personal preferences he decided against lowering the hem. He would of course have to shave his legs.

Gathering up the dress, the electric razor and the cord, he went down to the toilet, feeling lovely as he descended the dark stairs naked. He returned to the attic in order to walk down the steps again, this time with the razor and the dress around his neck, and his hands behind him spreading his buttocks. He laughed with delight as the chill air kissed his asshole. In the old days, when he was a Jew, he'd adored being rimmed.

He shaved his legs to just above his knees—believing

that a little hair under a skirt was exciting—and then powdered them to cut their sickly blue-white.

He tried on the dress. To accommodate his shoulders he was obliged to leave most of the little buttons in the back undone, and this brought the neckline down to where the hair on his chest began. He trimmed himself clean with the razor.

He considered shaving the whole of his chest, but decided against it, enjoying as he did the secret feeling of the satin pressing down the hair. All of his skin tingled. His nipples hardened.

He went upstairs and, without any hesitation, chose the rest of his outfit. The dress knew just what it wanted: the mask of a middle-aged woman with a longish but aristocratic nose, a red fright wig, a white straw picture hat with a bunch of cherries on the band, a pair of white shoes with three-inch heels. John Anthony lowered the brim down over one eye. He felt shabby-genteel and hoped he was going to Rumpelmayer's, though he was a little worried it might be Schrafft's.

He found a chipped white patent leather pocketbook, threw a camel's hair coat over his shoulders, and drew on a pair of white cotton gloves that were split open in most of their seams.

Holding on with both hands to the banister, he clop-clopped in the dark down the two flights of stairs. He searched the street carefully from the windows and, seeing there was no one about, stepped out and locked the Aviary door behind him. Dropping the keys in his bag, he walked south, turned a corner and, to his surprise, began heading fast for the Bowery. He could barely keep up with his feet.

The first bar he passed had its doors open and John Anthony felt suddenly dry. The woman he was tonight had a taste for boilermakers of which he disapproved. Wasn't she going uptown after all? Even to Schrafft's? Even to Child's? She walked north on the east side of the street, teasing herself with the raw smell of beer and whiskey. Oh well, things could have been worse. Remember the blue serge suit with the heavy key chain who hung around the Fulton fish market all of one night eating raw mackerel.

"Veronica, I thought you were dead!"

"I? Dead?" She turned and saw old Julie English sitting on the curb. "I spent some time on the Riviera as a guest of Dortelle's. You know Dortelle of course, at least by reputation."

"Well, you're back just in time for the cold. Brrr!" said Julie and tried to haul himself up from the curb. "Come on, give us a hand. My hoofs are as bad as ever."

Veronica considered, then thought, Why not, the past is the past, and helped her old lover to rise on his small broken feet. He gave her rump a squeeze as he stood swaying alongside her.

"Cut it out or I'll give you a push and you'll land where you land. In the dirt, the very dirt you made me eat."

"Ve-ro-ni-caaaaa," he sang sadly.

"No, none of that. I did my time chasing you. And to

the day I die my only regret will be that I wasn't there when the train passed over your toes."

"You always did look prettiest when you got a little mad, like now," he said, knowing how to soothe her.

Then he took her arm and they walked down the Bowery together as in olden times. Supported by her, there was something delicate and charming in his walk, for he wobbled along the balls of his feet like a dancer. She hoped she wouldn't fall in love with him again.

The effort of strolling two blocks cost Julie a moan.

"Why don't we stop and have a drink?" Veronica said.

"I'm somewhat short on cash."

"I can stand you a beer. There's Fraser's across the street. Remember?"

"We can't go there, you know. It's full of rich perverts now and they only sell beer by the bottle."

"The way things change in New York in so short a time! You turn your head for a minute, and when you look back, you don't know where you are."

"Only the places change, sweetheart. Not the people." He gave her arm a meaningful squeeze. "Let's go into MacDonald's. That hasn't changed. Not the place nor the people."

Veronica seated herself at a table near the window and haughtily ignored the greetings shouted to her from the bar. Then she pulled a dollar out of her bag and gave it to Julie.

"A double rye and a beer for me. And a beer for yourself. And the correct change, please."

"Can't I have a whiskey, sweetheart?"

"No, it'll make you miserable all night, imagining your toes hurt."

"That doesn't happen any more, Veronica. It hasn't happened in years."

"Like you said, Julie. Only the places change, not the people. You can have a beer and that's all."

So as not to have to watch Julie hobble over to the bar, she crossed her legs, fixed her hat and looked hard out the window. The vampires were returning with the coming of the cold, just as they used to do. She saw one sitting on the Salvation Army marquee, spreading his huge bat wings to scare her as he caught her glance. She stuck out her tongue at him and wagged a finger, for nothing scared her any more except the full moon when she dreaded turning into a werewolf. And even this not so much as formerly, because Veronica was frank with herself and, as unflattering as the thought was, she knew that any werewolf must just as much dread turning into her.

Julie put the glasses on the table, and Veronica quickly drank the double rye, feeling it shout hurrah into all the sleepy corners of her body. Things woke in her. She sipped the beer more slowly and grew morose. Tears came into her eyes and she remembered her lost children. They must be faring badly in the big cold world.

"Are those tears, Veronica?" asked Julie, pulling his chair close to her. "Are you crying, my little lambie sweetheart?"

"Ah, the human estate, the human estate," she whimpered.

"We are getting older, love. There's no escaping it. Maybe we ought to join forces again. I can still get Tiny Tim up from time to time. We could get ourselves a little room maybe and get a few pensions or some welfare. And eating at the Aviary, think of the money we'd save. For trips, like in the old days. What do you think, Veronica?"

Veronica didn't answer, for she was enjoying a metaphysical anguish. She was staring out the window at the passersby. She saw a fat Negress, a well-dress middle-aged couple carrying a camera, a policeman, a few bums, a Chinaman, a bunch of rich perverts on their way to Fraser's. They passed before her eyes as revelations. She saw, she comprehended them in their assembled reality: masked, costumed, wigged, their arms and legs stitched on, their eyes, noses and mouths splashed on by paint or ink, dumped on like candied fruit on marshmallow faces. Ah, terrible terrible humanity!

Exalted by her vision, she turned to Julie and said, "Forgive me, Father, for I have sinned."

"Have you, sweetheart?"

"I have done it all," she cried with a sweep of her arm. "All of it, all the horror, and the hideous little joys. I am the mother of God. Out of my womb has grown the tree of illusion."

"Oh, I guessed that long ago, Veronica," he said slyly, for he knew that to disagree with her now would only drive her into ecstasy. "It's what makes your life so hard. It's a terrible burden for one pair of shoulders to bear."

Slowly and heavily, she nodded, and her vision closed. Veronica felt void.

42

Twins! Tomtom Jim cut the second cord and thrust his knife up proudly. Two perfect tan boys yelling at the tops of their lungs.

Under a banyan tree on the bank of the River Smahna, Mary lay in a nest of soft grass, Baby in her arms as always. He sucked her dark nipple, but his eyes were fixed south, watching with unmistakable cynicism the miracle of birth. And his expression didn't change when Tomtom Jim wrapped him in mosquito netting and laid him in the grass.

"Two bright new sons for you, honey," said Tomtom Jim, giving the babies to Mary. "You have the best little farm in the world."

Mary flushed with pleasure and hugged her sons. "It's not so much the farm as the farmer."

Tomtom Jim whooped joyously and unbuttoned the button on his fly. "It's not so much the farmer as the plow—and the big black horse that pulls it." He did a belly dance, flinging the horse and the plow around. He danced along the jungle edge and along the river bank, going as far as the big wooden sign that said: EQUATOR.

Mary laughed so much that she began to ache. "Stop it!" she gasped. "Stop! I'm afraid everything will fall out of me."

The happy father sat down beside the happy mother. He stroked her hair and she stroked his cock. As she did this, she was filled with wonder at the strangeness of life.

"Isn't it all amazing?" Mary said.

Tomtom Jim was in harmony with her thoughts. "Amazing," he agreed, panting.

They stroked in silence.

Presently Mary said, "How's Baby?"

"He's all right. He's just there next to you in the grass."

Tomtom Jim smiled and tried hard to conceal his disgust, for he didn't want to be an old-fashioned stepfather.

"And where's Bijou? "

"I guess around playing somewhere. I've been pretty busy myself, you know. But you don't have to worry about Bijou. She can take care of herself."

No sooner had Tomtom Jim uttered these words than a piercing cry echoed through the jungle.

"That's Bijou," Mary said, raising her head. "I'd know her voice anywhere."

"Just you sit tight, honey. I'll be right back."

He raced up the slope and disappeared among the giant banana trees.

Now, you must keep calm, Mary told herself, knowing that worry could curdle her milk. As she was still weak from delivery, however, she had no trouble keeping calm. She closed her eyes and fell asleep at once.

It was night when she woke. Millions of stars were flashing overhead, crickets were chirping, and a cool refreshing wind blew from the river. What a lovely place! Mary lifted herself on her elbows and turned her head, looking down the slope to the river. The water was filled with stars. Starlight swam like fishes. What a lovely lovely place! She lay down again and hugged the twins and thought how nice it would be if Tomtom Jim built them a house right here, right up into the middle of the banyan tree. She imagined how she would raise her children here and grow her own food. And Tomtom Jim always with her.

But then suddenly she remembered that they were pilgrims, wanderers—only she couldn't remember what it was that they were looking for. She didn't strain herself. Whatever it was, Tomtom Jim would remind her. He was the best husband and father in the world. He knew everything. Reassured, she looked up at the stars and, pretending that her husband lay beside her, soon fell asleep.

When she woke next, the sun was high overhead and drums were beating in the distance.

She had a splitting headache. She was hungry. The twins were crying on her breast. Only Baby seemed contented, laughing and gurgling inside the mosquito net. With a start, Mary realized that it must be nearly twenty-four hours since Bijou and Tomtom Jim had disappeared.

Those drums! Those heavy jungle drums! Mary tried to calm herself lest her milk go sour. She thought about what a lovely place this was and about a house and a farm. She rocked the crying twins. She could smell smoke now and she could also smell meat being roasted. Oh, how hungry she was!

The sound of a voice made her turn her head. Further up the river, an elderly couple were just stepping out of the jungle. The man held a camera in his hands. He posed the woman against the sign that said EQUATOR and then backed away to take the picture.

Mary waited until she heard the click of the camera and then wailed weakly, "Help, help me . . ."

The startled couple looked at her but didn't move.

"Help me. In the name of God, help me."

The woman seemed to slump against the sign that said EQUATOR and tears began rolling down her cheeks. The man was also crying. Then abruptly they locked arms and rushed into the jungle.

Mary screamed after them. And screamed and screamed.

But it was no use, and soon her screams turned into sobs as she thought about the hardness and the cruelty of life. After a while, she fell asleep again.

She next awoke into a raving pink dawn, a dawn of golden roses. All was silent, but it was the silence of Africa, full of receding songs, approaching cries, and the sound of things growing. With new strength and determination, Mary laid her twin sons on the grass under the net with Baby. Then she rose to her feet.

She listened and she sniffed. The drums of yesterday had stopped, and the smell of smoke and roasted meat was gone. She made her unsteady way up into the banana grove. It was still night among the trees, and it wasn't silent. Terrified, she picked her way through the grove. The smell of bananas was now everywhere around her, but even in the dark she could tell that the fruit was too high to reach.

Ahead, the darkness lifted, and she saw a clearing. As she was about to pass through the last trees, something moved at her right. She froze. Cautiously she rolled her eyes. It seemed to her that what she saw in the shadows were two globes hanging by long ropes from the branches of a banana tree. The globes were swaying. Probably they were balloons or something, and in any case not dangerous. So she decided not to investigate any further.

She entered the clearing.

In the twilight of this great space, Mary read signs of a feast, recently held. A fire still smoldered and bones were strewn about everywhere. Some of the bones still had a bit of meat and poor hungry Mary threw herself upon them and began gnawing. The flesh was tough and rather underdone, but she didn't feel fussy. Wouldn't Tomtom Jim laugh when she told him how she'd chewed away like a dog!

But where was he? And where was her darling Bijou? Should she cross the clearing and go deeper into the jungle? Now that she was't so hungry, she was more afraid. Besides her three sons lay behind her, weak and alone. What should she do?

While she stood in the clearing trying to make up her mind, the enormous roar of civilization suddenly filled up her ears. I must be going crazy, she thought. But no, she wasn't. All at once from out of the jungle came two jeeps and a truck followed by hundreds of people. About half of them were ordinary white people, wearing ordinary clothes, but the rest were big black practically naked men, wearing colored feathers on their heads and paint on their faces. If Tomtom Jim was among them, Mary couldn't see him.

Soon the clearing was ablaze with activity. The dead fire was lighted again. Enormous machines were unloaded from the truck and wheeled to the side. Wires were strung through the air. Everyone was busy and happy, and Mary enjoyed watching them. Although she kept getting into people's way nobody paid any attention to her.

At last a white man, who was so fat he could hardly move, turned to a nearly naked black man and said, "Who's that?"

He meant Mary.

"Search me," said the black man.

"Hey, lady," the fat man shouted. "Are you with the company?"

She shook her head. "I've lost my husband and my daughter, and I can't find them. You haven't seen a little dark girl or a big black man without paint and feathers, have you?"

"If you're not with the company, we'll have to ask you to leave the area. We start shooting right away."

"Goodbye," Mary said.

She went across the clearing and back in among the banana trees. Though it was already day now, she wasn't sure of her path through the jungle, and she stopped now and then, hoping to hear her sons crying. But there were no sounds, except the roar of civilization, and this too was beginning to fade. For a long time she went this way and that. Whenever the trees seemed strange, she backtracked so as not to go further astray.

The sun was high and hot when at last, with a cry of joy, Mary ran down the slope to her nest. But her cry turned into a wail of despair, for Baby lay all alone under the banyan tree. The twins were gone!

Wailing and shrieking, she tore along the river bank, no longer concerned for her milk. Like a madwoman, she howled for her sons. And soon she found them.

Somehow, wrapped together in the mosquito net,

they had rolled down the slope from the tree to the river. And there below were their little shrouded bodies, half in, half out of the water.

Mary's days of waiting turned into weeks. Her milk curdled but Baby of course didn't care. He would have suckled yogurt. The little mother herself was too distraught to think of food. A gnawing heart, a fevered brain. Only out of concern for Baby did Mary now and then tear up a handful of grass and feed herself.

43

Just before dawn, when the night was darkest, he was awakened by a tapping at the window.

"Let me in. Please help me. Let me in."

Was she a ghost? James Madison stared in fright and disbelief at the apparition on his fire escape. A luminous woman, glowing like the hands of a clock.

She tapped again. "Mercy, mercy. Please open the window. Let me in!"

She was plump and had long hair and the bosom bulging above the neck of her low-cut dress stood out like phosphorescent melons. His own nakedness embarrassed him and he pulled the blanket up to his chin.

Overhead someone was running on the roof of the

tenement. The woman looked up toward the roof, then in through the window again.

"Help me, I don't want to die," she cried.

James Madison lay still, the woman's eyes on his.

There was a thump on the roof, and the woman turned with a shriek and fled down the stairs of the fire escape. A moment later a man in a sailor suit passed by the window. He followed the woman down the iron stairs.

Nothing else happened. James Madison heard the fire escape creak and clank, but that was all. Yet he was so upset he couldn't fall asleep again. He kept listening for screams or shots. He listened for police sirens or whistles, and this made him think of John Doe who always grew rigid, whose eyes always grew frantic, at the howl of a siren, as if he were a hunted criminal. Maybe he was. After all, James Madison knew nothing of the life he led away from this apartment.

He was unhappy and troubled all through the day, and he thought about himself. He wondered if a lot of time had passed since that first evening when he had followed John Doe up the unfamiliar stairs, asking himself as he went, though not without gratitude, Where else is there to go? What else is there to do?

Yes, it must have been a very long time, months or years. Long enough for several harvests of the toilet paper flowers that grew across the floor. And during all these seasons, he hadn't once gone out—not even to the street.

He examined himself. He looked like a white pagoda,

for the substance had gone out of him and his skin hung in fold upon fold. He was weak. It occurred to him that he must die very soon, that he would simply fade into death, too weak to protest, too feeble to urge himself away. Yet the prospect didn't frighten him. He would perhaps close his eyes a little more forcefully than usual, the heavy lids shutting with a slam, and a few exhausting shocks would play through his blood, surprising his heart into using its last stores of energy. He would drop bloodlessly into death.

What would John Doe do when he found the white pagoda spread across the cot? Cry? Fling it out the window into the courtyard like empty beer bottles?

Late in the afternoon, James Madison rose and looked for his clothes. They were lying in a corner of the room, thick with dust and mold. He shook them out and slowly dressed himself, almost collapsing from the effort. The worn brown pants and the blue-and-gold jacket hung on him, having become several sizes too large. His shoes looked as though they had been strangled, their tongues hanging out at the sides.

Dared he go out? Already his head buzzed, his limbs tingled, his heart groaned. There were noises in his ears, and bright transparent bubbles floated in front of his eyes. He went to the door, opened it. There were perhaps two yards across the landing to the stairs.

Falling to his knees, he crawled across the landing. Winded, he sat resting on the top step.

When at last he rose, he grabbed the banister with both his hands and gave all his powers of concentration over to the long descent. Step by painful step, he wended his way down into the world, growing dizzier and more breathless as he went.

It was still daylight when he touched bottom. He paused in his journey and leaned against the wall with the mailboxes.

"How hard it is to live," he said aloud.

Cautiously, he groped his way along the wall, then through the door and out into the street. A dozen blackjacks struck him on the head all at once. Gasping, he closed his eyes. When he opened them, he saw an ocean coming to a boil. Everything was swept together by the torrential waves. He couldn't distinguish the people from the cars, the buildings from the roar crushing in on his ears. He saw a single and colossal tide of madness, with everything caught in it. The world swirled and struggled, drowning. While he had been high and dry up in the fifth-floor apartment, the universe had opened all its dams. There were no longer any rivers or navigable currents. There were no directions. If he took just one more step, he would be swept from the shore and flung into the amorphous oceanic upheaval.

Unexpectedly, a way opened, a gentle stream appeared. It rippled out of the flood like a sunny shallow mountain brook. It was John Doe with a box of chocolates under his arm and a cigar butt clamped between his teeth. Seeing James Madison, he made a movement of surprise, then frowned; but he barely hesitated before starting up the stairs.

Oh beautiful stream! Oh divine current!

44

Of all the places he had now secretly gone to, none seemed more wonderful to him than that soft exquisite country where John Doe's journey ended every night. He was glad John Doe had this in his life, for everything else he had was grassless and ugly. James Madison knew, since he'd followed him into all the avenues and alleys of his day. Great stone office buildings, stiff little restaurants with stiff little people marching in and out, subways, museums where dead air pressed down on his head, movies, public toilets. No wonder John Doe was so tortured, so full of bitter hate. It was better to lie around in a tenement taking pills all day and growing feebler and flabbier than to have to live among those stones and machines.

Poor John Doe. Poor Johnnie.

But Johnnie wasn't poor at night. At night he had the world. And consequently James Madison had it as well. And he didn't need to steal taxi money out of John Doe's wallet any more to get there, because he had discovered the train. Every evening now, whether or not John Doe had come to visit him, James Madison walked uptown to the station and proudly showed his commuter's ticket to the guard at Track 4.

He liked to get there toward the end of rush hour, when the trains were still jammed but the passengers more exhausted. He loved getting crushed in the aisles and jabbed in the ribs, to have his toes stepped on and newspapers poked in his eyes. A dreamlike voyage through the darkening countryside, with villages springing into light. He was beginning to recognize certain groves of trees like new friends, impatient to get to know them better. And platform attendants. And gasoline stations on the highway across from the railroad. He was even beginning to recognize a few of the passengers. One of them, a tall old man in a homburg, nodded to him now.

Of course, when he took the one o'clock train back to the city each night, there were hardly any other passengers. But he could have a seat then and watch the world pass his window while he thought about the evening he had spent. He could doze and murmur prayers of thanks for all God and John Doe were giving him.

So James Madison spent the next to last days of his

life contentedly, perhaps even happily. And if at last he came to a sorrowful end, he had no one to blame but himself. He got greedy. He wanted more than God and John Doe were able to grant him.

The end began like all the other nights, with James Madison walking the frosty but enchanted mile from the station to the house. Overhead the sky was almost bursting at the seams with all those hysterical stars screaming for attention. James Madison smiled and waved, threw kisses at them, applauded loudly. Under his thrilled feet, dry leaves broke open in a crunching autumnal chorus. His heart pounded its unbearable joy. At each corner, in the lamplight, big fragrant trees whirled out of the dark, tossing their glorious golden heads.

And the smells! Of freshly washed sheets, of newly cut grass, of logs burning, of hills rolling, of peace and contentment. Peace and contentment, a pair of subtly scented flowers that bloomed here every night.

On John Doe's white picket fence was hung a wooden plaque and a small yellow light that never went off. In antique gilt lettering the plaque said: *Chez Vous*— PROP. T. S. FERGUSON. *Chez moi,* James Madison told himself and felt if possible an even greater rush of joy.

He unlatched the gate, stroked it, petted it, then pushed it open and listened to the homely creak of the hinges. He went up the flagstone path and across the lawn, around the side of the house to the lighted windows.

There were no guests tonight, thank God. He didn't much like company; they made him feel neglected. Still, that wasn't nearly so bad as when the Does went out for the evening and he had no one to look at but the baby sitter, an elderly lady whose snores made the windows rattle. John Doe was sitting in the big easy chair, looking bored and disgusted. James Madison smiled and puckered his lips.

He was watching television. He uncrossed his legs and since he wore nothing but underpants, one of his balls came popping out on the right, shiny and red. John Doe scratched it distractedly, and James Madison hugged himself, though this wasn't the first time he'd seen Johnnie's balls. Once he'd seen his cock as well, when Johnnie had an itch or something and pulled it out right in front of his wife and examined it.

On the table alongside his chair was an ashtray with a lit cigar in it, a bottle of whiskey, a container of milk, a bowl of ice cubes, and a glass. Just like the apartment, except for the ice. James Madison swelled with fierce fiery love. Oh if he could hold John Doe in his arms, kiss him once, lay his head in his lap! James Madison knew that what he saw before him, idly scratching its testicle, was not merely a man but the thread and meaning of his life.

In a blue woolen bathrobe, Mrs. Doe appeared, carrying a bowl of roses and ferns. Now why didn't I ever think of that? James Madison asked himself. It would make the apartment so much prettier. Of course there were the toilet paper flowers stained with—James Madison interrupted himself. He mustn't think this way, it was wrong. John Doe needed them both, his wife and his lover, the roses and the toilet paper.

Mrs. Doe set the flowers on the breakfront and primped them like hair. Then she went and sat on the arm of her husband's chair. She laughed at something on the television screen. John Doe's face became more sullen. Mrs. Doe reached down playfully and tickled the exposed testicle. Her husband slapped her hand away and fixed himself another drink. He was in a bad mood tonight.

What am I doing out here? James Madison suddenly asked himself. Why aren't I in there where I belong? He couldn't remember the answer, and worse he couldn't remember why for so many nights he'd stood looking in from outside. Why, I must have been mad, he said, and turning, he went across the lawn and up the pillared porch. He was surprised and amused to find he didn't have the key in any of his pockets.

So he pressed the doorbell, and the oriental chimes tonkled. A tonk-a-lonk, low and muffled, rolling across a carpeted floor. Soon the brass lantern was lighted, and the door swung open.

"I seem to have lost my key," he said.

Mrs. Doe stood there with her mouth open.

"It's me," said James Madison, his voice cracking. "It's just old me."

The door closed with a slam.

He stood facing the polished walnut. When the door opened again, John Doe, in his white boxer shorts, looked out, turned pale, and seemed about to faint.

"Are you sick?" James Madison asked.

With a hand on the doorpost, John Doe pulled himself together. Anger flashed across his face, but passed so quickly that James Madison never even trembled.

And then his eyes were gentle. "Wait. I'll be right out. Just stand here for one minute."

The door closed again, but didn't slam.

James Madison walked down the steps to the lawn. Putting both hands over his mouth, he began to sob, loudly but not recklessly. The stars cried with him, their warm tears dropping on his forehead and in his hair.

John Doe returned and led him to the car. While the motor warmed up, John Doe put his arms around James Madison and kissed his cheek.

"I wish I had tears," he whispered.

James Madison, who had plenty of them, rested his head on John Doe's shoulder.

"I love you," he said and fell asleep still crying.

When he awoke he was happy, because there was a drizzle on the roof of the car, and inside it was dry and safe.

"You know I won't be able to see you any more," said John Doe.

Looking out the window, James Madison saw that they were on Madison Street. In spite of the drizzle, an orange cat was smelling around at the garbage pails.

But there were no people on the street. There was only street.

"Did you hear what I said? "

"Yes."

"Of course you can keep the apartment. I'll go on sending in the rent, and I'll send you some money every week so you can get yourself on your feet again. I'll put it in an envelope and mail it to John Doe. The name's on the mailbox. Oh, the key! I can't think where the key is."

"The little key with lots of little bumps?"

John Doe was surprised. "You know where it is?"

"On the shelf over the sink. I didn't know it was for the mailbox."

"You'll take care of yourself, won't you? "

"You too."

"And I hope you won't do anything foolish—like come out to my house again."

"Don't worry," he said reaching in his pocket and fondling the commuter's ticket.

John Doe looked quickly up and down the street. "Here, you can touch it if you want. I'm sorry I made such a thing about it."

"Doesn't matter," said James Madison and, too humble and too proud to show that he was hurt, touched it.

"That feels good."

"I'm glad."

The meeting was then concluded and James Madison

stood on the street watching the car disappear. Then he walked over to the small triangle of public park rammed in among the projects. The park itself was deserted but two Negro boys watched him from across the street. He didn't worry about it. All they could do was kill him, and this didn't seem important.

The skinny unleafed trees looked desolate. The night was wet and foggy, but the drizzle had gone. James Madison sat down on a bench. He merely sat. He merely sat. He merely sat. He merely sat. He merely sat.

45

Dragging himself from tree to tree, he sang, "My father died for me."

He was a tall scrawny man now with graying hair and hollow cheeks and wild purple eyes that beheld meaning everywhere. As he lurched through the twilit jungle, his clothes in shreds, blood seeping out of his ulcered legs and torn arms, Xavier's brain hummed vague significant music. The story of Noah went through his mind, and closing his eyes he remembered in agony that he had uncovered his father's nakedness. He crushed a date palm to his breast and tensed himself, waiting for the flood, waiting for the cleansing waters to rise and scoop him out of the trees, fling him into the sky.

But the waters didn't come, and his agony ebbed, and

he looked up at the deep blue evening sky that hung in tassels from the branches overhead. Where was the rainbow? Where was the arc of colors, the covenant marking the end of the flood and the beginning of peace? His eyes bulged and pounded, but no rainbow appeared.

Muttering "My father died for me," he freed himself from the date palm and limped slowly off to another, trailing blood across the jungle floor.

Because he was mad, the universe flew to him and collected itself in his brain where it blazed like a sun, sang like a canary, glowed like a sweet Saharan lemon. All was one in him, but it was painful. In his arms he now held Lot's daughter, a pillar of salt with dates growing out of her head like a Medusa. She who had buggered the angels, fucked her father, turned back to watch the city of sin follow her out of the underworld. Xavier comforted her and forgave her.

"Our fathers died for us," he sang.

The melodies in his mind became clearer and purer. He heard the fine thin pipings of Pan. Nymphs and sprites, the green grassy gods in the trees and the vines, swayed with the pipings, began to dance.

Xavier flung himself in among the dancers, gave himself from one nymph to the other, each of whom whirled him through the orchids in a dizzying pirouette, kissed him with their wet young mouths and let him go. As he spun through the trees, he saw a clearing in the distance, and the pipings of Pan grew shrill, called out his name.

"My father, my father," he cried.

For who but the gentle father who died for him would be there squatting among the dozing beasts and sleeping birds, piping a tune to their dreams?

"My father," he wailed and bolted into the clearing.

The startled birds lifted themselves in a rush to the sky and the animals fled in among the trees. The black man laid his pipe down.

Without the music, the universe dimmed, began falling apart and leaving him.

"Don't stop playing," cried Xavier and threw himself to his knees before the black man. "Papa, Papa, I must have music."

Something flashed in his father's hand and made a ticking sound. "Father Time," Xavier cooed, remembering the overgrown Lot, the drunk incestuous Lot, where ghostly niggers lurked with knives in eternal night, under the ancient elevated line.

With a smile, his father reached for him, and Xavier went into his arms.

An acute icy sharpness illuminated Xavier's belly, then it turned into trumpets. The universe flew in again, collecting itself in his guts. Happily, he stretched himself out at his father's feet.

Before he closed his eyes, he heard the trumpets and the pipings of Pan and the songs of the wood nymphs all gathering together in his belly. All the melodies joined in the beginning of an unbroken dream. They joined with the approaching patter of animal feet and the rush of wings as the hungry birds descended.

223

46

A cruel fanged wind was blowing through the harsh
night streets of midtown Manhattan, and poor Mary
Poorpoor in her threadbare coat, remnant of another,
better life, wandered aimless and alone. Alone, that is,
exept for little Emilio, her comfort and her cross. Mary
thanked God he didn't mind the furious winds nor the
indifferent city, and that he lay gurgling in his blanket,
happy to be pressed against his mother's breasts.

Where was Mary to go next? She looked around. Excitement was in the air. People with painted faces and
pretty clothes hurried hither and thither. Enormous
hooting cars struggled to pass each other, or simply to
move. Through the windows of bars and restaurants she
saw happy people eating and drinking. Lights blinked

and blazed and flashed. It was a joyous town, Mary thought with a sigh, and only she was sad.

She made her way further west where the streets were darker and less crowded, the people drabber, the buildings uglier and without the promise of entertainment. It seemed more appropriate to her here, more in harmony with the wretched quality of her life.

As she crossed Eleventh Avenue, she heard a blast of joyous music, and despite the quality of her life, decided to follow the sound. It came from a big old-fashioned building of red stone that stood in the middle of the block. Alongside the building was a parking lot jammed with tremendous black limousines that had chauffeurs waiting in them.

There were windows at the front of the building, but they were all heavily curtained. So Mary went along the wall that sided on the parking lot, and to her delight found a window that was wide open. Standing on her toes, she peered in and saw a brilliantly light room. A masked ball was in progress.

This must be fairyland, she thought, and her arms and legs began to tingle strangely. She felt she was on the verge of a memory, but the feeling soon faded and she burst into merry laughter. The dancers were gorgeously dressed. The women wore evening gowns that must have weighed a ton apiece, so encrusted were they with jewels and sequins, and gold and silver thread. They wore feathers in their hair and furs around their necks. Most of them were masked, some elaborately, some with only thin black strips across the eyes.

The men were less spectacular than the women, for they were more simply and soberly dressed. Nonetheless their evening clothes were splendid, and one man wore a red velvet jacket with emerald studs. And everyone was dancing and laughing and drinking champagne out of tall crystal goblets.

Suddenly a handsome unmasked rather elderly gentleman in a plain black tuxedo walked by the window. Mary felt chilly and sneezed. She sneezed so loudly that the man was startled. He went to the window and looked down.

"Why, hello there," he said.

"How do you do, sir."

"What are you doing out there in the cold? "

"I—I was just watching the party. I hope that isn't wrong. I didn't mean to disturb anybody."

"It's not wrong at all. Why don't you come in and join us?"

"Oh, I couldn't do that. Not in these rags."

"Why not? They're lovely rags. Besides, it wouldn't matter a bit. Probably nobody would even—Good Lord!" the gentleman exclaimed. "Is that a baby you have there?"

Little Mary nodded her head and large tears sprang into her eyes, tears as lovely as the costumes at the party. Crying, she felt well dressed.

She said, "Yes, sir. It is my poor fatherless son, Emilio."

"Emilio?" the gentleman cried, leaning so far out the window that Mary took a step back, afraid he would fall. "Emilio? Is that his name? What an extraordinary coincidence! That's my name too. Just you wait there a minute. Now, don't move. Just you wait there. Promise?"

Hesitantly, Mary promised.

The gentleman disappeared from the window, and in a moment he was standing alongside Mary.

"Poor little Emilio," he whispered. "And poor pretty little mother."

"My name is Mary," said Mary, curtsying.

The gentleman threw his head back and laughed. "Ho ho ho!" laughed the gentleman, hugging Mary. "Your name can't be Mary. Mary is a boy's name."

What kind of joke is that? Mary wondered, but she smiled to be polite.

To make a long story short, soon Mary was sitting beside the gentleman in the back of his limousine, and he was saying, "Home, Johnson," to the chauffeur.

"The *garçonnière*, sir?"

"I said, Home."

"You mean the mansion, Mr. Emilio?"

"Are you deaf tonight, Johnson?"

The car backed out of the parking lot and in a moment was up on the elevated highway, heading north.

Somewhat later, when the Hudson River was on one side of them, and Sing Sing Prison on the other, the gentleman hugged Mary to his big soft chest and put her hand to his crotch, which was empty and very wet. With a cry of alarm Mary pulled her hand away and held it up in the moonlight to see if there was blood.

"Ah, yes, my dear," said Emilio. "You are entering a strange new world."

"That party—"

Emilio nodded. "Yes, little Mary. Yes. Does that shock you very much?"

Mary breathed heavily. "Not really *very* much. Only a little." Slowly, she smiled. "But I'm sure I could get used to it."

"That's my girl," said Emilio, patting her hand and very gently lifting it and placing it once more into the soggy serge.

47

Here was the beginning of the world—a silvery ever-green forest filled with smoky gray light. The wood of birth, of murder, of suicide. From its granite floor, boulders stuck out, stood up, rose spreading into hills. Colorless mold seeped across the stone like lace, like webs, like fur, like snot, like gism. Life thickened. Life slithered. Life gnawed. With horror and nausea James Madison watched life crawl across the granite floor while a fine phlegmy fuzz crept slowly over his skin.

Things ate. Inside the mold, ferns were snapping savagely, biting holes through which they could lift into the air their exquisite feathers and gracefully woven fans. Jellies and powders fell lightly on the ferns, dug themselves in, began sucking.

Larger things took root among the smaller. There lived grasses and brambles and bush and finally tree. And in the highest branches of the tallest pine, clouds of white moss hung on by their teeth, and chewed. Mold ate the trees, and the trees ate each other. Trees burst out of trees, panting for breath like conquerors. They dug their roots into each other and lived triumphantly.

All through the wood were the sounds of splitting and cracking, snapping and gnawing. Everywhere was the sweet glorious smell of life bursting and rotting. The forest floor grew soft and thick with death.

And here was where James Madison had come to die. Here, where the world was in eternal beginning, would he die of a heart as broken as an evergreen. Soon he will lay himself down on the granite or the mold or the soft rotting pine needles and become one with the beginning of things. In ending, he will begin a fern, a tree, perhaps a flower. His blood will flow green in the silvery forest.

As he wandered through the wood, preparing himself for his death, he came by chance upon a small clearing, and in this clearing stood a telephone booth. He thought of his mother and longed to say goodbye. So he put a dime in the slot and dialed the operator.

He said, "I would like to call Mrs. Mary Madison in New York City. And would you please reverse the charges?"

"Who shall I say is calling, sir?" Her thin voice, composed of wires, electricity and love, so enchanted him

that he said "What?" in order to hear her speak again.
"Who shall I say is calling, sir?" she repeated.

"James Madison."

"Thank you, Mr. Madison. Hold on a minute, sir."

Wires touched, electricity danced, love stretched its long arm. There was a buzzing.

"Hello," said Mama.

"Mrs. Madison?" the operator asked.

"Who?"

"Are you Mrs. Madison?"

There was a long silence before Mama spoke. "Who are you?" she said.

"I'm the operator, madam. I have a collect call from a Mr. James Madison in Silverwood Lake. Will you accept the charges?"

"He's not here."

The operator giggled. "Mr. Madison is calling you, madam. Will you accept the charges?"

James Madison suddenly spoke, his voice hoarse. "Mama, it's me—your son."

"Who?" she screamed. "Who?"

The operator said, "Mr. Madison, I'm sorry but I'll have to ask you not to speak until Mrs. Madison accepts the charges. Mrs. Madison, your son is calling you from Silverwood Lake. Will you accept the charges?"

There was a pause. Grudgingly she asked, "How much are the charges?"

The operator giggled again, making James Madison blush.

"We won't know that," the operator said, "until you've finished the conversation. There is, however, a minimum charge of eighty-five cents for the first three minutes."

"Eighty-five cents?" she yelled. "Where is he—in Europe?"

"Mama, Mommy, it's me, your baby."

"I'm sorry, Mr. Madison," said the operator, "but I'll have to disconnect you until Mrs. Madison agrees to accept the charges. Will you hold on, please?"

There was a click, and then nothing. He put the receiver back on its hook.

The forest was still at its meal.

"Wait for me," he cried to the mold and the fern.

Behind him, back in the clearing, the telephone had begun ringing, and though he could hear it, it was now simply a part of the forest smell and the smoky gray light, apprehensible but unanswerable.

James Madison stopped at a big dead pine out of whose heart a new young tree was growing. He snapped a branch off the older tree. It was like a lance—strong, silver, bare, pointed. He put its rough base on the ground and its point against his belly. It dug in just a little through the flab. He took a deep breath, then impaled himself.

He fell on his side screaming with the branch sticking out of him. He could scream as loud as he wanted to now, so he screamed the way he'd wanted to all his life. Until the trees shook. Until the granite opened. Until every feeder in the forest paused in its meal to wonder.

The telephone was still ringing, and he heard it, orchestrated with his screams. All the wood was filled with the music, so much so, in fact, that before losing consciousness, James Madison gave a gasp of dismay and asked himself, Why didn't I think of dancing instead?

48

John Anthony threw his hands up in disgust and went to hide behind the Christmas tree where, looking out between the cotton balls and tinfoil birds pasted on the window, he saw that it was snowing. Big heavy flakes shimmered like a curtain in front of the lamppost, and they were already beginning to cover the walk. It would be a white Christmas after all, or more probably a gray one, the whole city turning into a warm vat of soupy slush. But tonight would be white or even silver—if there was a moon—and it would be lovely when all the Birds stood caroling under the walls of Sing Sing Penitentiary.

He lost himself now in imagining that this year he could organize the singers more successfully, with more authority. They would stand in a compact unit, the snow falling in their hair, the moonlight turning them silver, their voices rising as one voice up to the barred windows. The prisoners would shout down through the bars and wave handkerchiefs and strike matches so that the Birds could know their songs were heard, and heard gratefully. Elegant passersby, with bundles of last-minute shopping in their arms, would stop and, tears in their eyes, join with his smelly tattered Birds in singing up to the oppressed, the forsaken. No, no, they would all sing, you have not been forgotten!

And when the warden would send his men out to try and shut the carolers up, they'd sing twice as loud, for God was with them. God was a lamb who'd suffered too!

A scream made John Anthony turn and peer through the tinseled branches. The Birds were still tearing furiously at the cartons of prettily wrapped candies, ties and kerchiefs sent down from various convents. One woman had blood all over her face. John Anthony muttered a prayer for the salvation of his Birds' greedy souls. A war was going on, and the Cardinal was trying desperately to make peace. They were all hitting each other, pulling things out of one another's hands, pounding, kicking, slapping, scratching.

Only two people were at peace. Xavier, smiling his beautiful smile, walked around the Recreation Room plugging sticks of smoking incense into cracks in the wall. John Anthony watched him gratefully. With so many Birds gathered together, the place truly stank.

The other peaceful person was crazy old Genevieve who, wearing a yellow chiffon party dress, sat on the stairs leading up to the attic. She clapped her hands and cackled, watching the war. "Get him," she shrieked. "Tear his fucking heart out!" Her feet went up in the air and John Anthony saw under her skirt. Ties and kerchiefs were tied up the length of both legs.

When Xavier finished with the incense, he went and sat on the stairs alongside Genevieve. She threw her arms around him and kissed him on the cheek. Feeling jealous, John Anthony turned to look out at the snow again.

Presently the war ended, the gifts now torn apart or eaten. John Anthony came out of hiding.

"All those who will sing with us, get going!" he yelled. "The rest of you get out. We're closing up. We'll meet at the train station."

In his blue earmuffs and duffel coat, Xavier stood aside and waited by the tree while the Birds filed down the stairs, through the dining room and out into the street. His eyes met John Anthony's, and they smiled at each other.

"Look at this mess," said John Anthony, nervously.

"Never mind. We can come back and clean up later, can't we?"

They went downstairs together. The Birds had begun singing "Joy to the World" as they marched down the street. John Anthony locked the Aviary door, and then linked arms tightly with Xavier.

They walked in the snow and in the moonlight. Practicing how he would project his voice up at the prison, Xavier threw his golden head back, opened wide his mouth and joined the distant carolers in their song. Snow dissolved on his warm pink tongue.

49

Ismael was even uglier now than Tommy. His glazed green eyes were like leaves of sugared mint stuck on a huge toasted marshmallow. Every three seconds, with a tick-tick, his artificial eyelids fell and rose, bathing the cornea.

But he and Tommy were together at last and happy as could be in the back room of the Rosas' apartment. They had their own electric cooker and did all their own housekeeping. The kids never bothered them; in fact, they ran and hid when either Ismael or Tommy came out for water or to go to the toilet. During the day they played casino, took pills and smoked pot. At night Tommy read aloud from the Book of Job. They made a lot of love, even more than in the old days, even perhaps more passionately.

And they had a brand-new mask which John Anthony created for them while Ismael was still in the hospital. This mask was of Ismael's face as it had been before the tragedy. Often Tommy put it on and knelt before his beloved and said, "Look into the mirror, darling. Look at your own loveliness." Tommy also wore the mask when they went to bed. Occasionally, though not often, he had to wear it on the back of his head rather than the front, for he could only get fucked while lying on his belly.

A couple of times a week, suddenly, inexplicably, a rush of overpowering hatred seized Ismael's heart and, throwing on his hooded black denim jacket, he raced from the room, the apartment, down the tenement stairs, out into the street. With his hood up and his head lowered, he walked rapidly over to Broadway, toward the subway station. And he took up his post in the dark doorway of a shoe store closed for the night. There, he waited, as he was waiting now, his eyelids ticking.

He heard footsteps. Someone was approaching. Lifting his head and pushing his hood aside, Ismael reached out his hand.

The man gasped. (They always did.) His eyeballs popped and he turned pale. (That always happened.) He hunted quickly through his pockets and pulled out a five-dollar bill. The look in his horrified eyes said "Forgive me" as he crammed the money into Ismael's hand.

Within a half hour, he had collected twenty dollars. That was enough; besides the hatred had gone out of him now. He left the doorway and started home again. As he walked, he felt his body beginning to quiver with laughter, his heart swelling with it. They think it's me, he said to himself, holding his mouth so as not to stain the streets with his laughter. They think it's me.

AFTERWORD by Diana Athill

It is possible that I am the only person in the United Kingdom who remembers Alfred Chester and his books: what he wrote was too strange to attract a large readership, and I and my colleagues at André Deutsch Ltd. did not overcome this problem. But he remains the most remarkable person I met through publishing, and I—like his friends in the United States who, since his death in 1971, have been finding new readers for him—continue to think and talk about knowing him as one of my most important experiences.

He was twenty-six when I first met him, in 1956, the year we published his novel *Jamie Is My Heart's Desire* and his stories *Here Be Dragons*. First impressions? The very first was probably of ugliness—he wore a wig, his brows and eyelids were hairless, his eyes were pale, he was dumpy—but immediately after that came his openness and funniness. It didn't take me long to become fond of Alfred's appearance.

He also inspired awe, partly because of his prose and partly because of his personality. Alfred wore a wig, but never a mask: there he sat, being Alfred, and there was nothing anyone could do about it. He was as compactly himself as a piece of quartz.

He had come to London from Paris, where he had been kicking up his heels in green meadows of freedom from his conventional, even philistine, Jewish family in Brooklyn. Already brilliant young New Yorkers such as Susan Sontag and Cynthia Ozick, who had known him when they were students together, were eyeing him nervously as one who might be going to outshine them, but he had needed to get away. And now he was in a state of first-novel euphoria, ready to enjoy whatever and whoever happened. Meeting him, whether alone or at parties, reminded me of the excitement and alarm felt by Tolstoy's Natasha Rostov on meeting her seducer and knowing at once that between her and this man there were none of the usual barriers. Something like that shock of sexual accessibility can exist on the level of friendship: an instant recognition that with this person nothing need be hidden. I felt this with Alfred (though there was a small dark pit of secrecy in the middle of the openness: I would never have spoken to him about his wig).

On his second visit he was with his lover, a very handsome young pianist called Arthur. When I went to supper with them in the cave-like flat that they had rented or borrowed, Arthur spent much time gazing yearningly at a portrait of Liszt, and I wondered whether Alfred was husband or wife in this ménage (heterosexuals are always trying to type-cast homosexuals). I decided eventually that, on that evening, anyway, what he mostly was was Mother.

That was the first time he talked to me about identity, explaining how painful it was not to have one—to lack a basic "I" and to exist only as a sequence of behaviors. He asked if I had a basic and continuous sense of identity, and I was tempted to say "No" because my freedom from anxiety seemed shallow and uninteresting compared with the condition he was claiming. I think I put the temptation aside because I didn't take him seriously. How could quartz-like Alfred feel, even for a second, that he had no basic identity?

Nevertheless I remember that long-ago talk very clearly. Perhaps I am being wise after the event, but it seems to me there was a slight judder of uneasiness under the surface that fixed it in my head.

Through 1956 and '57 we exchanged letters, and one of his contained a passage that now seems obviously deranged.

I was running away from the police, through Luxembourg which is incredibly beautiful (a valley in the midst of a city), then to Brussels and back to Paris in thirty-six hours without sleep only to find that no one was chasing me after all. Unless they are being incredibly clever. You see, I'll be able to do things like that when I finish my book.

That sounds like paranoia. And how does the last sentence connect with the first two? But I was not much disturbed by this letter at the time. The rest of it was cheerful and normal, and the sobriety of my own life compared with Alfred's must have made me assume that his might well include mystifying events.

A letter of mine dated July 1959 reminds me that one of his London visits ended when he disappeared without a word.

> ... at one time, a long time ago, there was an extraordinary panic in London. John Davenport kept calling me and Elizabeth Montagu kept calling me and I kept calling J. D. and E. M. and they kept calling each other and at one point an excursion was organised to Archway to confirm that you really had vanished and were not lying there sick unto death, or dead, or were not under arrest. After a while we said to each other "Look, if any of those things had happened we'd have heard *somehow*. Wherever he is he must be all right." So we gave up.

It was about a year after this disappearance that a visiting New Yorker let fall that Alfred was back in New York, and gave me the address to which I sent the above, whereupon Alfred replied that yes indeed, he'd become fed up with Greece and was now installed in a Greenwich Village apartment "with a *roof garden!*" And that was where I next saw him when I was on a business visit to New York: in almost unfurnished rooms above the theatre on Sullivan Street, where I found our friendship in good health.

Alfred had to lead the way up the stairs because he was feuding with the landlord, who had taken to leaving brooms and buckets in the darkness to trip him and send him crashing through the frail and wobbly banisters. As we climbed he described the feud with great relish. It was still daylight, so he took me right to the top to show me the roof garden—the heat-softened asphalt of the roof's surface, thickly studded with dog turds. Dutifully I leaned over the parapet to admire the view and the freshness of the breeze, but I was shocked. Dogs are quasi-sacred in my family. I had been raised in the understanding that they don't ask to belong to people, and so, given that we have taken them over for our own pleasure, it is our duty not only to love them but to recognize their nature and treat them accordingly. Never have I denied a dog exercise and the chance to shit in decent comfort away from its lair—adult dogs, except for half-witted ones, dislike fouling their own quarters. I saw soon enough that Alfred's beloved Columbine and Skoura, whom he had rescued in Greece, were a barbaric pair, perfectly happy to shit on the roof—and indeed on the floors, and the mattresses that lay on the floors to serve as beds. They had never been house-trained, and Skoura, anyway, was half-witted. But still I was disconcerted that Alfred was prepared to inflict such a life on his dogs.

It was dark by the time we sat down by candlelight (the

electricity may have been cut off) to eat mushrooms in sour cream and some excellent steak, and the dim light concentrated on the carefully arranged table disguised the room's bareness and dirt. Halfway through the meal we heard someone coming up the stairs. Alfred hushed me and blew out the candles. A knock; a shuffling, breathing pause; another knock; another pause; then the visitor retreated. When Alfred relit the candles he was looking smug. "I know what *that* was. A boy I don't want to see anymore."

That led to talk of his unhappiness. Arthur, the most serious and long lasting of all his loves, had left him. He was trying to force himself into an austere acceptance of solitude, but like a fool kept on hoping, kept on falling into situations that ended in disappointment, or worse. The boy on the stairs was the latest disappointment, a chance pick-up who turned out to be inadequate. I said: "But Alfred, dear heart, what makes you think it *likely* that someone you pick up in a urinal will instantly turn into your own true love?" He replied condescendingly that I had no sense of romance.

My two favorite memories of New York were given me by Alfred during my visit: he showed me the only pleasure in the city which could still be had for a nickel, and he took me to Coney Island. The nickel pleasure was riding the Staten Island ferry there and back on a single fare, which meant hiding instead of landing at the end of the outward journey. Early on a summer evening, when the watery light and the ting-tong of a bell on a marker-buoy almost turned Manhattan into Venice, it was indeed a charming thing to do. And Coney Island was beautiful too, the water sleepy as it lapped the dun-colored sand, the sound of the boardwalk underfoot evoking past summers that seemed—mysteriously—to have been experienced by me. Sitting on the beach, we watched the white flower of the parachute jump opening and floating down, opening and floating down . . . Alfred teased me to make the jump but I'm a coward about fairground thrills, and jibbed. He too was afraid, and told stories about famous accidents. He showed me where, when he was a child, he used to climb down into the secret runways under the boardwalk, and instructed me in methods of cheating so that this or that could be seen or done without paying. He was fond and proud of the child who used to play truant there and had become so expert at exploiting the place's delights, and as we sat beside each other in the subway, going home, I felt more comfortably accepted by New York than I had ever done before. I don't remember him ever talking about the pleasures of being an *enfant terrible* reviewer, capable of causing a considerable frisson in literary New York, which he was at that time.

Being the publisher of someone whose books are good but don't sell is an uncomfortable business. Partly you feel guilt (did we miss chances? could we have done this or that more effectively?) and partly irritation (does he really expect us to disregard all commercial considerations for the sake of his book?). Alfred gained a reputation for persecuting his publishers and agents with irrational demands, but with us he was never more than tetchy, and most of the uneasiness I felt came from my own disappointment rather than from his bullying. In England he was all but overlooked: a few reviewers made perfunctory acknowledgment of his cleverness and the unusual nature of his imagination, but many more failed to mention him. Our fiction list was well thought of by literary editors, and I had written them personal letters about Alfred. I was driven to wondering whether the favor we were in had backfired: had they—or some of them—taken against his work and decided that it would be kinder to us not to review it at all, rather than to review it badly? Only John Davenport, a good critic who had become Alfred's friend out of admiration for his writing, spoke out with perceptive enthusiasm.

When I was in New York, soon after our Sullivan Street dinner, I spent an evening with Alfred and his then agent during which he prophesied that his next book, the story collection *Behold Goliath*, would sell a million copies. His agent and I joined in trying to persuade him to modify his grandiose expectations, which earned us a sharp scolding for our negative attitude. This—when our dismal lack of success with the book became clear—made me dread the prospect of furious letters from him. No such letters ever came, then or at any other time. He had been teasing us, and had taken those million copies no more seriously than we had.

I have forgotten when Alfred moved to Morocco and whether he told me why he was doing so (Paul Bowles, who thrived there, had suggested it at a party in New

York). The first letter that I still have with a Tangier address was written soon after the publication in England of *Behold Goliath*, early in 1965.

DEAR RAT

Why haven't you written?

Why didn't you let me know about publication?

Why haven't you sent me copies?

Why haven't you sent me reviews?

I will not make you suffer by asking why you didn't use the Burroughs quote, though I would like you to volunteer an explanation. I hope you will write me by return of post.

I'm coming to England, either driving in my trusty little Austin or by plane which terrifies me. I'm coming with my Moroccan boyfriend, and the real reason for the trip is to get his foot operated on. He has a spur, an excrescence of bone on the left heel, due to a rheumatic process. I'm afraid of doctors here. But please keep this a secret as they probably won't let us into England if they find out . . . I would appreciate it if you would check up on surgeons, bone surgeons or orthopedic specialists. I have some money so it doesn't have to be the health insurance thing, though that would help . . . They always used to fuss about me at the frontier, so there's bound to be a fuss about Dris. I am going to tell them that we are going to be your guests over the summer. I hope this is okay with you (for me to say so, not for us to stay) and that if they phone you or anything you will say yes it's true. Please reply at once.

Oh, I don't know if Norman mentioned it, but I don't wear a wig any more. [Norman Glass was an English writer he met in Morocco, who had called me when he returned to London to give me news of Alfred.] I thought I'd better tell you in advance so you don't go into shock. I like it better this way, but I'm still somewhat self-conscious.

Edward [Field] says I must give you and Monique Nathan [Alfred's editor at Editions du Seuil, Paris] a copy of *The Exquisite Corpse* immediately. [Jason] Epstein [of Random House] says: "I doubt very much that I can publish the book in a way that will be satisfactory to you, and I don't want to compound our joint disappointment in *Goliath*. The other reason has to do with the book itself. I recognize its brilliance—or more accurately I recognize *your* brilliance—but I confess that I'm baffled by your intentions, and I'm concerned that I would not know how to present the book effectively. I don't mean that for me the book didn't work; simply that it worked in ways I only partly understood. Or in ways that suggest it is more a poem than a novel, though whether this distinction clarifies anything is a puzzle."

The book is too simple for him. It reads like a children's book and requires innocence of a reader. Imagine asking Jason Epstein to be innocent . . .

Will let you see it when I come. PLEASE REPLY BY RETURN OF POST. Love.

My answer:

I did tell you publication date, I have sent you copies—or rather, copies were sent, as is customary, to your agent (if A. M. Heath is still your agent —they are on paper. I called them this morning and they said they'd post your six copies today, and I don't know why they haven't done this before). Here are copies of the main reviews [my lack of comment makes their disappointing nature evident]. And I didn't put the Burroughs quote on the jacket because no one in Sales wanted me to, Burroughs being thought of here except by the few as dangerously far out and obscene, and they not wanting to present you as more for the few than you are. Should have told you this. Sorry.

I am enclosing a letter of invitation in case it may be useful with the visa people or at frontiers. It's marvellous that you are coming . . .

Your quote from Jason Epstein made me laugh —there's a nervous publisher backing against a wall if ever there was one. I was also, of course, scared by his reaction because there is nothing more twitch-inducing than waiting for something to come in which you know is going to be unlike anything else, for fear that it is going to be so unlike that one will have hideous forebodings about its fate. I'm dying to read it. Hurrah hurrah that you'll soon be here. Love.

His answer, written in a mellow mood, ended with the words: "As for *The Exquisite Corpse* being unlike, yes, it is probably the most unlike book you've read since childhood. And probably, also, the most delicious."

I could not have rejected *The Exquisite Corpse*, because it seemed—still seems—to me to draw the reader into itself with irresistible seductions. Alfred was right: you must read it as a child in that you must read it simply for what happens next, without trying to impose "inner meanings" on it. The title comes from the game called in England "Consequences"—it was the Surrealists who gave it the more exotic name. Do people still play it? A small group of people take a sheet of paper, the first person writes the opening line of a miniature story, then folds the paper so that the next person can't see what he has written; the next person writes the next line, and folds—and so on to the last person, whose line must start "and the consequence was . . ." Unfold the paper and you have a nonsense story that is often delightfully bizarre. You can do it with drawing, as well as with words: I can still remember a sublime monster produced that way by my cousins and me when I was a child, far more astonishing than anything any of us could have thought up on our own, yet perfectly convincing. Alfred followed the "consequences" principle—it's as though the paper were folded between each chapter, and when people you have already met reappear you are not always sure that they are the same people—perhaps the name has been given to someone else? Sometimes appalling or obscene things happen to them (I still find it hard to take the scene in which the character called Xavier watches his papa dying). Often it is monstrously funny. In no way is the writing "difficult." There is nothing experimental about the syntax; you are not expected to pick up veiled references or make subtle associations; and there can never be a moment's doubt about what is happening to the characters. The writing—so natural, so spontaneous-feeling, so precise—makes them, as Alfred claimed, delicious. The book's strangeness lies entirely in the events, as it does in a fairy-story, remote though Alfred's events are (and they could hardly be remoter) from those of Hans Andersen.

I was captivated, but two things disturbed me. The first was that we would be no more able than Jason Epstein to turn this extremely "unlike" book into a best-seller, so Alfred was bound to be disappointed. And the second was that it left me feeling "one inch madder, and it would have been too mad."

This was something to do with the contrast between the perfection and airiness of the writing and the wildness of the events. The easy elegance, the wit, the sweet reason of the style are at the service of humor, yes; of inventiveness, yes; but also of something fierce and frightening. A fierce—an aggressive—despair? If aggressive despair is screamed and thumped at you it is painful, but it makes sense. When it is flipped at you lightly, almost playfully . . . Well, it doesn't make nonsense, because nothing so lucid could be called nonsensical, but (like Jason Epstein) I don't know for sure what it *does* make. I am captivated, but I am uneasy. I am uneasy, but I am captivated. The balance wobbles and comes to rest on the side of captivation. I use the present tense because I have just reread it for the first time in years, and reacted to it exactly as I did at the first reading.

When Alfred arrived with Dris he was wigless. He looked impressive—face, scalp, ears, neck all tanned evenly by the Moroccan sun. Although he had already given me permission to comment by mentioning it in a letter, I had to screw up my courage in order to congratulate him on his appearance. I don't think I am inventing the shyly happy expression on his face as he accepted the compliment. As I learned later, a childhood illness had left him hairless, and having to wear a wig was the most terrible thing in his life—an affliction loaded almost beyond bearing with humiliation and rage. Throwing it off had taken great courage. It was vastly important event to him, an act of self-creation.

Morocco, I thought, had given him a new calm and freedom, and he agreed. The version he gave me of the place was all liberation and gentleness: you could smoke delicious kif there as naturally as English people drink tea; no strict line was drawn between hetero- and homosexual love; and you didn't have to wear a wig—you could be wholly yourself. I rejoiced for him that he had found the place he needed.

A couple of days later he brought Dris to dinner at my place—handsome, cheerful Dris, with whom I could communicate only by smiling because I have no Spanish. After dinner Alfred sent him into the kitchen to wash the dishes, which shocked me until they had both convinced me that it was dull for him to sit listening to incomprehensible English. Soon Dris stuck his head round the door and offered me his younger brother—he thought it wrong that I should have no one to do my housework. Alfred advised against it, saying that the boy was beautiful but a handful and that Dris constantly had to chivvy him out of louche bars. Dris himself had become a model of respectability now that he had a loving and reliable American, and Alfred—so he said—would one day be the guest of honor at Dris's wedding. That would be recognized in Morocco as the proper conclusion of their relationship, and probably Dris's wife would do Alfred's laundry while their children would be like family for him. It sounded idyllic.

The high point of the evening was the story of their adventures on their drive to England, told with parentheses in Spanish so that Dris could participate. Alfred had crashed the car in France. When the police came Dris was lying on the ground with blood on his head. It was really only a scratch but it looked much worse and Dris was groaning and rolling up his eyes so that only the whites were visible. Yes, yes, Dris intervened, sparkling with delight, with Alfred interpreting in his wake. He had suddenly remembered that a friend of his had been in an accident in France, and was taken to hospital, and when

255

he got there *he was given all his meals for free!* So Dris decided in a flash to get to hospital where he would save Alfred money by getting fed, and also—this was the inspiration that filled him with glee—by complaining piteously about his foot, as though it had been hurt in the accident, he would make them X-ray his foot, as well as feed him, so that Alfred would not have to pay for an X-ray in London. Unfortunately this brilliant wheeze came to nothing because he was not allowed to smoke in the ward, so before he could be X-rayed he became too fed up to endure it, and walked out. It was pure luck, Alfred said, that they had run into each other as they wandered the streets.

Alfred's gloss to the story was that the police and ambulance men had been fussing around so that Dris had no chance to explain his plan. Alfred had seen him whisked away without knowing where to, and had spent a day and a night adrift, wondering how the hell he was going to find Dris—and, indeed, whether Dris was still alive. Later this struck me as odd. It is not difficult to ask a policeman where an ambulance is going, or to find a hospital. I supposed he must have been stoned out of his mind at the time of the accident, although I had never seen him more than mildly high and he was always careful to give me the impression that mildly high was as far as he went. I sometimes thought that Alfred tended to see me as slightly Jane-Austenish, which caused him to keep his less Jane-Austenish side averted from my view.

I didn't see much of him on that visit. He was affectionate and easy, but after a couple of hours I would know that I was becoming an inhibiting presence. I always assumed that he wanted to bring out the kif, which I didn't use, so I would say goodnight and leave, feeling that the real evening was starting up behind me. (I was unaware then that he also used other drugs.) Dris's foot remained a mystery. He saw a doctor, he did not have an operation, someone told me that the spur had been diagnosed as a result of gonorrhea; and Alfred, when questioned, was vague, as though the matter had become unimportant.

Another of his long silences ensued. I suppose there must have been communication of some sort between us—I knew he was still in Morocco—but there was nothing memorable, and I was not surprised because we had no habit of correspondence. A letter from Alfred usually meant that either he or a manuscript was about to appear; and my life was so full that I don't think I was aware of how very long this silence was.

It was two years later that he again appeared—out of the blue. As I came into the office one morning the receptionist behind her keyboard half rose from her chair and signaled that someone was waiting to see me. I peeked round the corner, and there was Alfred, sitting in a hunched position, staring into space. "Oh my God, trouble" . . . the reaction was instantaneous, although his attitude might, I suppose, have been attributed to weariness.

I welcomed him and took him to my room, asking the usual questions and getting the information that he was on his way back to Morocco from New York and had stopped off because he needed to see a dentist. Would I find him one, and would I give him some typing to do so that he could earn a little money while he was here? Of course I would. And then, in a tone that indicated that this was the visit's real purpose: "Will you call the Prime Minister and tell him to stop it?"

Stop what?

The voices.

I must not attempt dialogue or I will start cheating. The voices had been driving him mad. They gave him no peace, and the most dreadful thing about them was that they, not he, had written every word of his work. Did I see how appalling it was: learning that he had *never* existed? And even Dris was on their side. They often came at night, very loud, jeering at him. Dris, in bed beside him, *must* have heard them. He could only be lying when he insisted that he didn't. It was not really for the money that Alfred needed the typing, it was because it might drown the voices.

He had been to New York, where he had beaten up his mother. Before bolting to New York he had attacked Dris, too, because he insisted there were no voices. He was in London now because of what I had told him in Fez. But I had never been to Fez. Oh yes I had—last week. Alarm became more specific because of the stony way he looked at me: I saw that it was possible to become one of "them," an enemy, at any moment. I said cautiously that this Fez business puzzled me, because certainly my *physical* self had been in London last week.

I told him I had never met the Prime Minister (Harold Wilson it was then), and would not be put through to him if I called him, but that I could approach a Member of Parliament if that would do. I also told him that I was sure the voices were a delusion. He replied that he could understand my disbelief, and that I thought he was mad, so could I not in return understand that to him the voices were real, "as real as a bus going down the street"? Yes, I could grant that, which seemed to help. It enabled him to make a bargain with me. If I proved that I was taking him seriously by approaching an MP, he would take me seriously enough to see a doctor.

That settled, things began to go with astonishing slickness. When I called my dentist I got through in seconds, and he was able to see Alfred that afternoon; it also turned out that we had in the office a manuscript that genuinely needed to be retyped. Both of these pieces of luck seemed providential, because I was sure that Alfred would have interpreted delay or difficulty as obstruction. (He kept all his appointments with the dentist, behaving normally while there, and he typed the manuscript faultlessly.)

After he had gone I sat there shaking: it would not have been very much more of a shock if I had come across someone dead. Then I pulled myself together and went to discuss the crisis with the person in the office most likely to know something about madness, who recommended calling the Tavistock Clinic for advice. At that time R. D. Laing and David Cooper were in their heyday, and someone at the clinic suggested that I should get in touch with Laing. He was away, so his secretary passed me on to Cooper.

Dr. Cooper agreed to see Alfred, told me that having offered to speak to an MP I must do so—it would be a bad mistake to cheat—and asked me who would be paying him. Alfred's family, I extemporized, hoping devoutly that it would not end by being me; and when, next day, I managed to speak to Alfred's brother in New York, he agreed. He sounded agitated, but a good deal nicer than Alfred's rare references to him had suggested. Then I called an MP of my acquaintance who said: "Are you out of *your* mind? If you knew the number of nuts we get, asking us to stop the voices . . ."

The thought of telling Alfred that afternoon that the MP would not play worried me enough for me to ask someone to stay within earshot of my room while he was with me. To my surprise he took the news calmly, and agreed to visit Dr. Cooper in spite of my failure. I began to see what I had been doing, talking to him in Fez: of all his friends I was probably the one most likely to think of madness in terms of illness, and of illness in terms of seeing a doctor, and because we saw little of each other I had not yet turned into an enemy. Alfred *wanted* to be proved wrong about the voices; he *wanted* someone to force him into treatment. I had been chosen as the person most likely to do that.

Nevertheless he could bring himself to visit Dr. Cooper only once, because "I don't like him, he looks like an Irish bookmaker." Cooper then volunteered to find a psychiatric social worker to talk him through this crisis, telling me that if this one could be overcome, Alfred would be less likely to experience another—perhaps. A pleasant, eager young man came to me for a briefing, then started to make regular visits to Alfred, who had found himself a room in a remote suburb—I think it was offered to him by friends, but I didn't know them. What Alfred thought of his conversations with the psychiatric social worker I never heard, but the young man told me that he felt privileged to be in communication with such a mind. I remember fearing that Alfred would draw the young man into his world before the young man could draw him back into ours.

Two, or perhaps three weeks went by, during which I called Alfred a couple of times—he sounded lifeless—but did not ask him to my place or visit him at his. I knew I ought to do so, but kept putting it off. This was my first experience of mental illness, and I felt without bearings in strange and dangerous territory. Having taken such practical steps as I was able to think of, I found to my shame that the mere thought of Alfred exhausted me and that my affection was not strong enough to overcome the exhaustion. Not yet . . . next week, perhaps . . . until the telephone rang and it was the psychiatric social worker reporting that Alfred had left for Morocco—and I felt a wave of guilty relief. Asked whether he was better, the young man sounded dubious: "He was able to make the decision, anyway." And after that I never heard from Alfred again.

I suppose it was his New York agent who sent me a copy of *The Foot*, his last novel, which has never been published in full, just in excerpts. There was wonderful stuff in it, particularly about his childhood and losing his hair—when the wig was first put on his head, he wrote, it was as though his skull had been split with an axe. But much of the book had gone over the edge into the time of the voices. After reading *The Foot* I saw why *The Exquisite Corpse* is so extraordinarily vivid: more than anyone had realized at the time, its strange events had been as real to Alfred "as a bus going down the street." He was already entering the dislocated reality of madness, but was still able to keep his hold on style: instead of leaving the reader flustered, on the edge of that reality, he could carry us into it. When he came to write *The Foot* his style had started to slither out of his grasp. By that time the sickness—which found such nourishment in the "liberation and gentleness" of Morocco, with its abundance of delicious kif—had won.

Without knowing it, Alfred left me a delightful legacy: his oldest and truest friend, the poet Edward Field. Some years ago Edward's tireless campaign to revive Alfred's reputation in the United States caused him to get in touch with me, and almost instantly he and his partner, the novelist Neil Derrick, took their place among my most treasured friends. It is Edward who told me about Alfred's last, sad years.

Back in Morocco, his behavior became so eccentric that he lost all his friends and alarmed the authorities. There was no way in which poor Dris could have helped him in his madness, but I don't know how long it took for this to become apparent, or whether the split was violent or just a tailing-off. I did hear, however, that Dris eventually went to work in a factory in Holland, and got married there.

Alfred was thrown out of Morocco, and moved with his dogs—new ones, not Columbine and Skoura—to Jerusalem, where he survived by becoming almost a hermit, still tormented by the voices and trying frantically to drown them with drink and drugs. I was shown by Edward what was probably the last thing he ever wrote: a piece intended to be published in a periodical as "A Letter from Israel." It was heartbreaking. Gone was the sparkle, gone the vitality, humor, and imagination. All it contained was baffled misery at his own loneliness and hopelessness. The madness, having won, had turned his writing—a bitter paradox—far more *ordinary* than it had ever been before. The world he was describing was no longer magical (magical in horror as well as in beauty), but was drab, cruel, boring—"mad" only in that the mundane and tedious persecutions to which he constantly believed himself subject were, to other people, obviously of his own making.

When he died—probably from heart failure brought on by drugs and alcohol—he was alone in a rented house that he hated. It is true that his death cannot be regretted, but feeling like that about the death of dear, amazing Alfred is horribly sad. However, other people are now joining Edward in keeping his writing alive in the United States: it is still a small movement, but it is a real one. May it thrive!

Alfred Chester was born September 7, 1928, in Brooklyn, New York, the youngest of three children of a Russian-born furrier and his wife. At the age of seven, a case of scarlet fever robbed him of his hair, even of his eyelashes, and for most of the rest of his life he wore a wig to mask his baldness. He attended yeshiva and Abraham Lincoln High School, and in 1949 received his B.A. from New York University. He then began graduate studies in English at Columbia, but after a year he moved to France, determined to become a writer. His first book, the collection of stories *Here Be Dragons*, was published in Paris in 1955. The following year his first novel, *Jamie Is My Heart's Desire*, was published in London by André Deutsch, marking the beginning of his friendship with editor Diana Athill. He returned to New York in 1960 and became one of the decade's most prolific and provocative literary journalists, publishing criticism in *Commentary*, *Partisan Review*, and *The New York Review of Books*. In 1963, at the suggestion of the writer-composer Paul Bowles, he moved to Morocco, where he found, for the first time, something like happiness. In 1964 he published a second collection of stories, *Behold Goliath*, and in 1967 his masterpiece, *The Exquisite Corpse*. His final years were characterized by wandering, alcoholism, drug addiction, and madness. He died in Jerusalem, alone and alienated from his friends, on August 2, 1971. His literary executor, Edward Field, has edited two posthumous collections, *Head of a Sad Angel: Stories 1953–1966* (1990) and *Looking for Genet: Literary Essays and Reviews* (1992), and is currently preparing an edition of his letters.